I0782437
A LESS THAN ZERO ROCK STAR ROMANCE
LIMITLESS
ENCORE
KAYLENE WINTER

LIMITLESS

ENCORE

Sensitivity Statement

Readers,

The Less Than Zero series dives into the highs and lows of rock-star life, inspired by the raw and real experiences of many in the music world. Across these stories, some characters face challenging themes, including abuse, sexual assault, mental health, fertility, and struggles with addiction. These topics are not universal to every character but are woven into the journeys of a few, which impact the entirety of the series.

At its heart, though, this series is about love—how it grows, heals, and transforms. Each couple's story ultimately leads to a well-deserved happily ever after, filled with passion, hope, and redemption. The band's journey supporting each other as "band brothers" also is a predominant theme throughout.

Please take a moment to reflect on your comfort with these themes before reading, and know that these stories are told with care and respect, sensitivity readers have vetted each one. Thank you for joining me on this emotional journey through love, life, and music.

With all my love,

Kaylene

Prologue

Beep. Beep. Beep.

Beep. Beep. Beep.

The annoying, repetitive sound started ten minutes ago. It's torture. Waiting here is torture. Hell, every single minute of each hour I've been here has been torture.

The worst of my life.

And the scariest. By a thousand miles.

Beep. Beep. Beep.

Argh. That fucking beeping noise is driving me insane.

I'm by myself and haven't dared leave this orange vinyl chair for nearly seven hours. I'm paralyzed. Terrified.

Being still isn't in my nature. Neither is being alone. I hate it.

I hate this.

But it's not like I have a choice. All I can do is stare through these floor-to-ceiling windows at downtown Seattle. Contemplate how much my life has imploded over the past couple of months. Wonder what's gonna happen to me and Alex once—not if—we get through this horrific setback.

Setback? No. Loss. Another loss.

What is taking so fucking long? I want to rewind the clock. Start the morning over with my free-spirited, fairy-nymph badass who's rocked my world since I was twenty-three and she was only eighteen. The woman's been in my bloodstream for over a decade. Just like I've been in hers.

What would I do without her?

Right now, I'm a live wire. Vulnerable. On edge. Panicking.

Utterly and truly.

I need to focus on something else. Anything else.

I resume looking out at the city and can't help but notice the condo building I used to live in is just a couple of blocks away. I bought it with the first big paycheck I received when my band, Less Than Zero, hit it big. Gawd, that's eight years ago now? At the time, I thought I was on top of the world.

I had no idea.

The true pinnacle for me is when Alex came back into my life.

She's not only the top of my world. She and Lena are my entire world.

I've never been this close to losing everything.

Who'd have thought I'd find true peace in the outdoors? With horses. A menagerie of animals. Not me. And yet, I can't imagine living any other way. My life is on our ranch now. That's my home. With my little girl and my fiancée and... For fuck's sake. Fiancée. What a stupid fucking title. Alex and I have been everything under the sun to each other. Acquaintances. Friends. Friends with benefits. Secret lovers. Madly in love. Parents. Engaged. Fuck. It's not enough, she should be my wife.

Why isn't she my wife?

I should have insisted long ago. Alex was the one who wanted to wait. All of her "we're married in spirit" bullshit. I always wanted more. She did too, but she was scared to commit to me fully. Afraid of...I don't know what, exactly.

I should have been more reassuring. More demonstrative. More...gawd. I don't know. I should have found some way to make her believe that I'm in this with her forever. That I'll never, ever leave her. No matter what. I told myself she's been through so much since we got engaged, I didn't want to nag her about a wedding and add to the pressure...

Fuck. I'm just making any excuse.

What if... No! I've got to snap out of this. Be positive. Send happy, positive vibes. Stay calm.

But how do you do that when the person you love most in the world is fighting for her life?

You don't. You can't. I'm going fucking nuts.

Wait. Wait. Wait.

Beep. Beep. Beep.

For fuck's sake. I can't just do nothing. I won't.

I spring up from my seat and stalk around the room like a madman. I'm sure I look like one. Wild hair. Wild eyes. Disheveled clothes. I don't give two fucks. I weave my way through dozens of ugly orange chairs, a brown vinyl couch, and past a bunch of nondescript landscape prints screwed into the walls.

I peer around the corner. There's nobody around. Figures. After all, we were trying to keep things private. When everything went down, I pulled some connections to clear the floor. Neither of us like to have people up in our business. We keep our shit to ourselves.

It's just... I wish I'd known how goddamn terrified I'd be here all on my own. I'm truly not able to hold it together for another minute. I should have known something by now. Maybe a progress report. Or an update. No one's telling me anything.

Beep. Beep. Beep.

I whip my head toward the sound. It's coming from down the hall. I decide to investigate. I must try to distract myself and get the crazy thoughts in my head to fucking stop. Hurriedly, I stride down the stark, bright hallway and around the corner. I'm nearly knocked over by Seamus McLoughlin, my bandmate Connor's youngest brother. He's one of the doctors on her case. When I found out he'd been assigned to Alex's care, it gave me such relief that someone I know would be with her.

Now, I want to fucking kill someone, and since he's here...

"Jace, I was just coming to get you." Seamus skids to a halt. "We need to talk."

I ignore him and try to move past. "No talking. I'm going to see her. You can't stop me."

"That's not possible right now." He presses his palm against my chest to stop my forward momentum. He's calm and businesslike, which further pisses me off. Nothing about his expression changes when he gestures back to the room I've been stewing in for hours. "Let's go have a chat."

"Seamus." I cock my head and fix him with what I hope is an intimidating glare. I've known this kid since he was thirteen, after all. It used to work well.

He shakes his head, unmoved. "Jace."

Beep. Beep. Beep.

My head whips around at the sound. The fucking noise is coming from the room Alex is in.

"What the fuck?" I lunge toward the door.

He places his hands on each shoulder to stop me and sighs. A flicker of emotion dances across his eyes.

"There's been a complication. Dr. Madison sent me outside to—"

"Complication? A fucking complication? What do you mean by that? After seven hours of hearing nothing, this is what you say to me?" My heart thuds in my chest.

He looks me directly in the eye. "We've been trying to save her life, Jace. All I can tell you is they're still working on her now."

After that, his lips keep moving but I can't hear what he's saying. The only thing that registers is white noise. Well, and utter and total blinding panic. I'm not prepared for this.

Won't ever be prepared for this.

Fuck. Why? Why did we mess with perfection? We were happy with our little family. Why couldn't we... Oh gawd. If I lose her...

When Seamus uncharacteristically pulls me into a bear hug, I nearly fall apart. He's never been a demonstrative dude. I pull away and gulp in some air. "Just tell me if she's going to make it."

"The team is doing everything they can." Seamus keeps eye contact, which I suppose is supposed to provide me with some level of comfort. "I promise."

His efforts are appreciated, except he's just spoken the least reassuring words in the history of words. I just stare at him. "How bad is it? Should I call anyone?"

"Yes. I would. Call her folks. Call yours. And your sister. I think having your family around you is important." He pats my back. "I should get back in there. We're giving her the best chance possible. You have my word."

With that, I watch him disappear back into the room. Like a robot, I dial my sister. She picks up on the first ring. "Jace?"

"It's Alex. I'm scared, Jen." My voice comes out as a sob as I explain what's going on and choke out the address. "Can you come?"

Without hesitation, my sister is the rock she's always been. "We'll catch the next ferry. Becca can stay with Lena. I'll call our folks and I'm happy to pick up Andrea. We'll all be there as soon as humanly possible."

With that task complete, I settle into what feels like a vortex of horror. My back slides down the wall and I pull my knees to my chest when my butt hits the ground.

Only one thing matters—being close to her now. If these are the last moments I have with the love of my life, I'm going to be just outside her door.

I bury my head into my forearms, clasp my hands together and do something I've never, ever done before.

I begin to pray.

Chapter One

One Year Earlier

GODDAMN BUNNIES.

They're friggin' everywhere. Little brown and tan garden-eating devils. I sink to my knees and survey the damage. All the cauliflower, peppers, arugula, and broccoli seedlings have been decimated. Ironically, a few of the carrots have survived, but for how long?

I make a decision as I brush off the dirt from my bare knees. Within thirty seconds, I burst through the front door with purpose. "Jace? Lena? Where are you guys?"

"Back here," my golden Viking drummer god yells from our little girl's bedroom. I arrive to the most precious scene. Helena sits on her daddy's lap sucking her thumb while he braids her hair into two pigtails. I sigh happily and lean against the door, watching them.

Whenever I see them together, I melt. Our little family is everything. Even though Lena isn't our biological child, she's ours in every sense of the word. Our baby. Our daughter. Our life.

Despite the strange circumstances which brought her into our lives, she adapted quickly. Even her caseworker marvels at how fast she's acclimated to our home. I know it's because she's meant to be with us, even if we don't share the same DNA.

Lena's bio mom was Jace's sorta-ex, Cassie, a fangirl he hooked up with before his band, Less Than Zero, made it big. He broke it off around the time my BFF Zoey and I met them. Zoey and Ty, LTZ's singer, fell in love at first sight.

Me? Gawd, I had such a huge crush on Jace, but he wasted no time in friend-zoning me. But I'm me and wasn't about to be denied. So, before he went on tour,

I seduced him. Gave him my V-card. Setting off our years-long on-and-off friends-with-benefits thing.

Yeah, it was that mind-blowing.

After quite a bit of back and forth, we attempted to be a committed couple one summer. We didn't tell anyone, so we had time to figure out our relationship for ourselves.

Turned out, I wasn't ready for it. I don't think he was either. It ended after I thought he'd gotten me pregnant. The test came up negative. Jace was super bummed. As for me? I'd always been honest with him. Rescuing animals was my thing. Not children.

Especially with a guy who toured ten months of the year.

With divergent dreams for our future, we went our separate ways. We lost touch for a long time. It sucked, because being with Jace ruined me for all other guys. No one could hold a candle to him. Not even close. That's when I realized how much I loved him. Really loved him.

When he and I reconnected at Coachella a couple years later, everything clicked back into place. Like destiny. He moved in with me here at the ranch and we were about to officially unveil our not-so-secret romance when the bottom fell out.

A couple of months before our reunion, that girl Cassie showed up at one of his shows. As Jace tells it, he was lonely and made the unfortunate decision to have dinner with the "manipulative cunt" and her equally "diabolical" sister. They roofied him. He woke up naked in bed with her the next day, with no memory of what happened. A year later, Cassie died in a car accident. Leaving behind a little girl, Helena, whose birth lined up perfectly with the roofie incident.

Just as he and I were finding our groove, Cassie's family threatened to extort Jace with a public paternity scandal. He kept it from me because they threatened me too. Not to mention, he was convinced I'd leave him if he was the girl's father.

I'm not gonna lie. The whole debacle nearly ended us forever. Because straight up, he should have told me. That being said, I'd been so adamant about never having kids. And as social media manager for his band, he was used to handling things with little input. So even though I understood where he was coming from, we came to a different understanding.

No more secrets.

Long story short, Jace's DNA didn't match. Instead of relief, to my own surprise, I was sad she wasn't his bio daughter. So was he. Both of us thought Helena deserved a lot better. Jace's dad got involved and helped him make her shitty biological family an offer they couldn't refuse.

We've never had a moment's regret of adopting our darling, perfect, almost-two-year-old daughter, who we now call Lena.

"Are you going to fill us in on today's plan?" I snap back to reality at the sound of Jace's voice. He cocks an eyebrow and kisses the back of Lena's head.

She reaches up and twists a lock of his long, blond hair around her finger and I can't help but laugh. "Lena, you've literally got your daddy wrapped around your finger." I stride over and smooth her hair. "What do you two think about getting a couple of cats?"

"Yah. Yah. I want kitty-cat." Lena claps her hands together. "Kitty-cat. Kitty-cat."

Jace can't help but laugh. "Did the bunnies strike again?"

I nod. "Yup."

No need to fill our daughter in on why we actually need a couple of cats. What she doesn't know won't hurt her.

An hour later, we're at the Kitsap Humane Society filling out the paperwork for Benjamin and Franklin, adorable year-old paired black-and-white barn cat siblings. I'm paying the fee when Lena shrieks happily, pointing at a German Shepherd puppy. "Pup-pup!"

Jace crouches down next to her. "Should we get a dog too, Lena?"

"Yah. I want this pup pup." Lena runs over to the kennel.

He looks up at me with a smirk. We've been talking about rescuing a dog ever since he moved in. The sable-brown dog with black markings is called Mitch. His soulful eyes connect directly with my heart. His abnormally long, pink tongue lolls out of the side of his mouth. I love him. I poke my finger through the cage and scratch his forehead between his eyes.

Mitch is meant to be with us. I know it instantly. There's a reason I have four million followers on Instagram. I'm an animal-rescuing badass. All of our animals on the ranch are either rescued or adopted.

"You're in heaven, aren't you?" Jace whispers in my ear.

I nod happily

"Daddy no kissy Mama." Lena burrows between us. We both laugh.

He waggles his brows at me before swooping Lena up onto his shoulders. We return to the adoption desk, and I point to Mitch. "We'd like to bring him with us too."

The girl handling the paperwork has Billie Eilish-inspired fluorescent-green hair. She looks me up and down, smacks her gum and nods at Jace. "Is he that drummer guy?"

"Nah," Jace drawls, not giving me time to answer. He prefers to downplay his fame. To stay in the LTZ background. Jace likes being incognito as much as possible. Of course, the man is drop-dead gorgeous. People notice him no matter what.

Green-hair girl eyes him skeptically but goes back to processing our pet adoption forms. Takes her sweet, precious time. Finally, we're piling Lena, the cats, and Mitch into the Range Rover. On the way home, Benjamin and Franklin wail like they're dying. Mitch howls in camaraderie. Lena giggles and mimics the howling. Gawd, Jace joins in too.

Needless to say, it's a loud ride back.

Once we load everybody into the house, I try to put a squiggly, squirmy Lena down for a nap. She whines and resists my efforts until I bring Mitch into her room. He promptly jumps up on the bed and curls up beside her, resting his head in the crook of her arm. Lena calms immediately and strokes his ear. Within minutes, they're both sound asleep. I tiptoe down the hall to join Jace in the spare bathroom where we're preparing the space for the kitties.

"Are you sure we should leave them in a bathroom?" Jace tilts his head toward me and tosses towels in the bathtub.

My nose is scrunched up into my brain when I glance up from my struggle with the lid on the automatic litter box.

"Aha!" I pump my fist in the air when it clamps into place. "Yeah, I'm totally sure. They'll be safe and isolated for a few days to get used to the smells of our house. I can work on some basic training with Mitch in the meantime. All of our new fur babies have great temperaments. I'm sure it will take a few days to introduce all of them. Doing this correctly will make life easier for us."

Jace leans over and wraps his hand around my nape. Pulls my face to his until our lips touch. "You're so fucking hot when you're bossy," he whispers against my mouth.

Moaning into our kiss, I grip his strong shoulders. Nuzzle the scruff on his jaw. Nip the cleft in his chin. Jace devours me like a starved man. His hand skims down my side to the hem of my black jersey dress. With one quick motion he flips it up, shoves my panties to the side and trails his fingers through my damp folds to my opening. I gasp when he plunges two digits inside me.

I buck my hips as he strokes my clit with his thumb. Squeak when he nibbles on my earlobe. It's mere seconds before I'm literally gushing against his hand. "I never knew cat litter would turn you on so much," he growls. "Oh, and if I'm not inside you within the next minute, I'm going to come in my pants."

Jace pulls his fingers out of me and places them against my lips. I suck them clean. Leaning up to his ear, I urge, "What are you waiting for?"

In the mad dash to our bedroom, Jace sheds his t-shirt, sneakers, socks, and jeans. I pull my dress over my head and step out of my drenched panties. He lunges toward me and cups my breasts with both hands and presses them together. My nipples stand at rapt attention. He thrums my nipples then pinches them a bit. "I want to fuck your tits, Poppy. Then I'm going to fuck you."

"Yesss," I hiss.

Lena's nap time is a scant hour, so we don't have time to waste. We've mastered the art of speedy, quiet sex since our daughter came into our lives.

I scramble to the bed and lie back against the pillows. Jace straddles my waist, reaches into the dresser, and squirts some CBD lube between my breasts and massages it in, paying special attention to my nipples. Tingles shoot directly to my pussy. Gawd, this lube is absolute euphoria. I squirm from the intensity each time he pulls and twists my tight buds.

"Your tits are what dreams are made of babe." Jace slathers lube on his engorged cock. Pumps it by dragging his strong hand slowly up and down his shaft to work the lube into his skin. His face contorts with pleasure as the gel begins to do its trick. I cup and press my breasts together, creating a tight channel, tight enough to thrust into. It's hot as hell watching the tip of his penis emerge from between my tits, millimeters from my lips.

He groans when I bend my neck so I can lick his crown on each pass. "Holy mother of Jesus, Poppy. Keep doing that. Ah, fuuuuuck."

My hips undulate in time to Jace's tempo. I desperately want to finger myself but can't because my hands are occupied. Ever the observant lover, Jace notices my distress and reaches one hand backward to rub my clit. The residue from the lube on his hand creates a magical tingle. "Ohmygawd," I whisper-shriek.

Jace withdraws his cock from my tits and works his way down my body, laving and kissing my skin until he literally buries his face in my pussy. Drags his tongue through my folds. Wiggles it against my clit. I'm a goner. I bite my knuckle to keep from crying out too loudly when I come like a freight train.

I'm surprised I don't break his jaw by how hard I clamp my thighs against his face.

"Put your cock in me. Now." I splay my knees wide. Jace obediently moves into position and presses my legs farther apart. That's where his obedience wanes. Instead, he impales me maddeningly slow. Inch by delicious inch. Rotates his hips. Snarls as he watches himself plunge in and out of me. I lean up on my elbows and peer down at our joined bodies so I, too, can enjoy the show.

"I. Fucking. Love. You." Jace's thumbs hold my pussy lips apart. My sensitive clit pokes up proudly. I reach between us and pinch it and rub. His hips buck into me with incredible power and speed. Our bodies slap to-gether, and he cries out, "Holy fuck, Poppy. I'm gonna—"

I surprise him by smacking my hand over his mouth because of a sound I hear on the baby monitor. He groans into my palm when he empties inside me. His eyebrow twitches. Then he blinks a few times. Finally, his eyes fly open when he becomes coherent enough to clue into what I heard.

Lena is babbling happily to Mitch through the baby monitor on my nightstand. "You my doggie, Mith. You my doggie."

"I'm sorry, I didn't want her to hear you," I say quietly before lowering my hand.

Jace arches an eyebrow. Eyes gleaming mischievous-ly, he drags his index finger down my body over my puckered nipples to my overly sensitive clit. He's still inside me when, with the perfect amount of pressure, he rubs it rapidly in tight circles. "You've got another, yeah?" he whispers, pressing the heel of his palm against my mound. The deliciously erotic pressure triggers an absolute tsunami of an orgasm. I grit my teeth just to keep from screaming out.

I'm breathless. Writhing. Spasming.

Worried.

It's so stupid. Lena can't possibly hear us, but I'm so hyper-focused on doing the right thing. I'd feel like the biggest loser if Lena's psyche was damaged by hearing me fuck her father.

The reality is, raising a child is nothing like working with animals, which I'm really good at. The truth is, I'm in a constant state of low-grade fear that I suck at motherhood. I have no clue what I'm doing. Um, ever.

I love Lena so much. I just don't want to screw her up…

Good gawd. My current inner dialogue reminds me of my best friend, Zoey. Too much over-thinking.

Jace is already dressed by the time I cycle through this particular round of my I'm a bad mother negative self-talk. He reaches down and caresses my face, reading my mind. "We always have time for sex, Poppy. Just because we love to fuck doesn't make us bad parents."

"I know, but—"

"Stop." He bends down to kiss me. "You're great with her. She loves you. All you have to do is relax. Take a breath. There's no perfect way to do this. At least that's what my mom says."

"My mom says the same thing." I relax against the pillows. Stick my lower lip out to blow an errant hair from my forehead.

"I'll get Lena up. We'll take Mitch outside for a pee and a walk to the barn and introduce him to the horses. That way you can take a little time for yourself." He kisses me again.

I nod, pressing my hand to his heart. Jace quirks his lips into a grin and turns to leave but I grab his hand. "I love you immensely, my sexy Viking man."

"Oh yeah? Then it's time to marry me." He winks and disappears to take care of our daughter.

I suck in a breath. Pull the covers up around me. Ever since we adopted Lena, he's relentless with the comments about getting married. The thing is a piece of paper doesn't mean anything.

I'd like for it to happen at some point. It's just...

After all the uncertainty we've navigated during our time together over the past decade, things are good now.

No, better than good.

Things are nearly perfect.

So...maybe we shouldn't rock the boat.

Chapter Two

One Month Later

I CAN'T TAKE MY eyes off her when she's around. It's been that way from the day I met her. Nothing's changed in nearly a decade.

She's Poppy. A perfect blend of stunning beauty and effortless chic. She smiles freely. Her wit is unmatched. I don't know anyone smarter. Or harder working. She loves with her whole heart and soul.

She's my fucking everything.

I find myself relishing each little gesture she makes. Like when she taps the toe of her black Frye boots on the floor every time she laughs. The way she always sticks her bottom lip out to blow phantom hairs off her face. Gawd, the huge smile that spreads across her lips when she's with our horses.

The way her eyes widen with awe every time I make her come.

The woman I love is a mixture of the absolute best contradictions. Worldly. Innocent. Sophisticated. Simple. Sexy. Sweet. The list goes on and on. I've got it bad.

I've had it bad for nearly a decade.

Currently, Alex is talking animatedly with my favorite women, all of whom are gathered around the kitchen island. It's the annual Deveraux end-of-summer BBQ at my family's house in Medina. Unfortunately, it's Seattle, so the weather isn't cooperating. When the rain started, we had to move things inside.

The women are an eclectic bunch. Ariana, Alex's older sister, is all conservative clothes and sensible shoes. She has a demanding job in London, so she's rarely in town. Jennifer, or "Jen," is the youngest of my sisters. We're the closest of my siblings. After all, she's just two years older than me. Becca is her girlfriend; they live at our ranch in the guest house. Jaylynn, my oldest sister, is married to Roberto. They both work for a software company and travel a lot for work. Jordan is in the middle. She's making an international name for herself as a tattoo artist. Most of my ink is her art.

Lucky for me, I have the family discount.

My pops and namesake, Jason, is a former tech executive at the world's most famous software company. I'm acutely aware I grew up with privilege. My childhood was spent on this ten-thousand-foot lakefront property in Seattle. None of my family are entitled, though. At least I don't think we are.

Pops always says he was in the right place at the right time. That might be true. But he's also a genius. He worked long hours when I was a kid and was able to retire as a fairly young man. Now he's the figurehead at one of Seattle's biggest investment groups. He works a grueling one day per month evaluating companies he wants to sink some of his vast fortune into. The rest of his time is spent serving on charitable boards. Or traveling with my mom.

Speaking of which, my mom, Grace, appears with Lena and hands her to me. "Someone wants her daddy." My daughter buries her face in my neck under my long hair. Shoves her thumb in her mouth and relaxes. I cup her tiny head with my palm and stroke her silky, golden-blonde locks. She may not be ours biologically, but somehow Lena looks exactly like a child Alex and I would make for real.

Wouldn't that be cool?

I push the thought out of my mind. I was surprised enough when Alex wanted to adopt Lena. She's a great mother. A natural. But I know the score. Animals are her jam. If Lena is our only child? I'm okay with it.

You can't improve upon perfection, after all.

"Did she like the playroom you set up?" I focus on the present. Like the fact my mom gutted a spare room in the house to create a kiddie wonderland for her first grandchild. Complete with an indoor gym and a mural of colorful jungle animals. Not to mention toys and games and a little snack area.

"I'm absolutely sure she's going to grow up to be a gymnast." Mom surveys the kitchen and waves at the group of women who are now beckoning her to join them.

I shoo her over. "Go. I've got her, Mom."

"My only son. How sweet you are with your daughter." Mom runs her palm down my cheek. "You make me proud."

I feel Lena go slack in my arms. She's already sound asleep. "My only mom." I lean into her hand. "I live to make you proud."

"Then stop acting like an idiot, and marry Alex," she stage whispers. Then sticks her tongue out at me and joins the women.

I fucking wish.

I've been dying to put a ring on Alex's finger. This year would be perfect timing. My band, Less Than Zero, is on hiatus. Two of my bandmates, Connor and Zane, are newly married and knee-deep in family stuff. Ty's engaged to Zoey. They're due home any day from wherever the fuck they're currently traveling.

My Alex isn't like the other women, though. She never mentions marriage. Never hints about getting engaged. I'll admit, I wish she were pushy. Especially now that we're parents. I need the commitment. I want what my parents have. Which is ironic considering I'm heading into my mid-thirties.

The piercing squeals of the women cause Lena to stir in my arms. Rather than risk her waking, I take her through the house outside to the expansive, covered back porch overlooking meticulously groomed gardens leading down to Lake Washington. It's quiet out here. The view of the water is unobstructed.

When I still lived at home, this was always where I'd chill.

Careful not to disturb my little girl, I sit on a plush lounger and lie back. Lena wiggles a bit but thankfully doesn't wake up. I gaze out at the curtain of rain falling on the deep-blue lake and feel at peace. My eyes are heavy. I'm dozing off when I hear footsteps approach.

I squeeze one eye open to see my pops plop down on the chair next to me and recline. He gestures with his thumb to inside the house. "There's a ton of estrogen in there. I figured I'd find you here."

"Well, where else would I be? This is our spot when it gets too squealy."

My dad shuts his eyes and smiles contentedly. "True that."

"Pops, it's been great having some time off. I miss spending time with you when I'm on the road so much."

"Me too, little dude. Me too. I'm glad you have some downtime. Not that adopting a toddler is downtime, of course. It's just sometimes it's necessary to take a break from work so your mind can catch up to your body. Figure out what's most important."

"Yeah. For sure. I needed it after all the band drama and my own shit to get settled with Alex and Lena." I swallow a lump that forms in my throat. "If I can be half as good a dad to Lena as you've been to all of us, I'll feel stellar about life."

His eyes spring open. "Uh, that's a really wonderful thing for you to say. I worked so much when you were little, I was hardly around. Your mom's the one who deserves all the credit."

"Yeah, Mom and my sisters are awesome. You're my rock though." It's the truth. Without his intervention, I'd still be tied up in some crazy paternity scandal. He's always on my side. He never appears stressed. He's just so...capable. I hope I'm growing into some version of him as I get older. I'm not there quite yet.

Dad reaches over and squeezes my wrist. "We're a lot alike. Same laid-back temperament. Same fierceness when backed into a corner. Same determination and drive."

"I wish." He's my favorite dude of all time. I'm lucky to have him; my bandmates haven't been as fortunate as me in the dad department.

"Can I tell you a secret?" he continues without waiting for an answer. "You'll come to learn as your family grows that there's no way to feel like you're a good parent on a day-to-day basis. It's scary shit."

Six months ago, I wouldn't have a clue what he's talking about. Now that we have Lena, though, I get it. "I never realized until we brought her home permanently how intense the responsibility is."

"Well, thank God you picked Alex as your partner. She's a keeper. You'll get through all of this together."

"Can I ask you something?" I look into my father's eyes, which are as piercing green as mine are.

"Sure."

"You like to tell the story of how long it took for Mom to agree to marry you. How you were patient. Waited. All that stuff. I'd like for Alex and me to get married, but she just doesn't seem into it." I fold my arm around Lena, who is still dozing away. "Should I officially propose and risk her saying no, or should I be patient and wait?"

Dad chuckles. "Jesus, maybe you should talk to your sisters about that one. But if you want my opinion, she's likely waiting for you to make a definitive move."

"I talk about getting married all the time," I protest.

"Do you though?" My dad cocks his brow. "I've heard you say you want to get married. It reminds me of how I used to talk about marriage with your mom before I wised up. One day after we'd been dating for a kazillion years, she told me she was leaving for a year to travel the world. The fear of losing the best thing that ever happened to me kicked me in the ass. I hope you don't need that sort of catalyst to kick your ass into proposing."

I try to recall if I've ever officially proposed. I squint over at him. "Um, I hear what you're saying but isn't it fucking obvious I'm in it for the long haul?"

"I don't see a ten-carat rock on her finger." Dad shuts his eyes and folds his arms across his chest.

Shit. Have I been that clueless? I thought Alex would laugh if I gave her a grand proposal like her best friend received. Connor and Ronni practically eloped. Zane and Fiona, well, they're in a category all their own. Still…

"Uh, Alex isn't Zoey. She'd hate a huge diamond ring. We're super low key."

"Sounds like you've got it all figured out then."

"Not really…" My mind is racing. Alex deserves the best. "What should I do?"

Dad keeps his eyes closed. "You know your girl. It doesn't have to be something crazy, just something that will mean a lot to her. You've got it in you. Didn't you get that poppy tattoo for her all those years ago? Didn't you rent a villa in Lake Como? All you've got to do is make a memory for her, J-bird."

"Yeah, but my previous grand gestures backfired," I mutter, semi-annoyed. "She's unique. In a category all her own."

"Well, then think unique. Trust your instinct." A couple minutes later, a soft snore indicates he's napping. I shut my eyes too and as I begin to drift off cuddling Lena, I try to remember all the times Alex and I have had actual conversations about getting married. A grand total of none. Only vague platitudes.

Huh. I realize my dad's on point.

I'm going to have to step up my game.

Because I've waited a long fucking time for Alex to commit to me.

I'm not letting her slip through my fingers ever again.

Chapter Three

One Month Later

GAWD, IT'S INSANE HOW bad my cramps have become over the past year.

For several months, the dull ache in my lower back indicates the start of it. The pain spreads into my hips and settles like an anvil into my lower belly a day or two later. By the next day, I'm not exaggerating when I say it feels like a million knives are stabbing me up through my vagina every time I take a step.

Or move. Or breathe.

Gahhhhhhhh...it's unbearable.

I release the death grip I have on the banister and sit on the stairs, frozen in pain. I can hear my mom, Jace, and Lena chattering away in the kitchen. There's one thing I must focus on. Getting myself upstairs where Mom keeps her blessed Tylenol with codeine tablets from Canada. They're the best option I have to manage this temporary agony so I can get on with my evening.

Nothing. And I mean nothing is going to keep me from this long-overdue date night with my man.

Still, it takes me about ten minutes to take the pills and wait for them to kick in.

"Poppy?" Twenty minutes later, Jace peers into my bedroom where I'm curled up in a ball on my childhood bed. "Are you okay?"

I look up at him. "Just bad cramps again, I took some 222s."

"Ah, my little druggie." He sits next to me and smooths my hair back. "I'm getting worried about how bad this is getting lately. I don't remember any of my sisters having this type of pain. Should you get it checked out?"

I roll on my back and stretch my legs out. "For the record, I'm taking over-the-counter medication from

Canada, I'm hardly a druggie. Usually, it works like a charm. I'm already feeling better."

Jace laughs and pokes me in the side. "Jeez. Sensitive much?"

I pout and stick my tongue out at him. I'm mature like that.

"Every time I'm in this room," he waggles his eyebrows," all I can think about is what we did in here when you seduced me."

My Lady Gaga posters have been torn down from the time when Jace took my virginity in this very bed. Mom converted it into a sweet little guest bedroom. I shift over on the bed and pat the space next to me. "Well, they were excellent firsts. So. Uh...do we have time for a quick orgasm? It's the best way to stave off my cramps."

"Sure, why don't I just tongue-fuck your pussy with your Mom and Lena downstairs. Should I leave the door ajar?" Jace bends over and kisses my temple. His long hair tickles my neck. I reach up and run my fingers through the dark-blond locks. Enjoy how his stubble scratches my cheek deliciously. My love's fierce, green eyes lock with mine and he smirks before swooping down to tongue-fuck my mouth. A consolation prize, sure. Still... hot. We savor each other for a second until a loud crash downstairs snaps us to attention.

I sit up. "What was that?"

"I'll go check it out. Which reminds me, the reason I came to find you is to say we need to leave in about ten minutes. Now five." He kisses me quickly and calls down to my mom as he bounds down the stairs. "Andrea, is everything okay?"

Taking stock of my situation, I realize the cramps have subsided. A quick trip to the bathroom allows me to verify my monthly visitor hasn't arrived yet. Thank gawd. In under five minutes, I throw on a lightweight lavender cotton maxi-dress. Add snazzy pieces of my favorite jewelry from my travel influencer days. Put on a little mascara. Dab on some lip gloss.

Voila. I'm ready.

When I make it down to the kitchen, Lena is seated on a barstool at the counter stirring something in a bowl. Jace is leaning over her staring at my mom's famous pie recipe book. Mom's beaming. "I thought I'd get my beautiful granddaughter and future son-in-law involved in the family business."

My breath hitches because we're still not engaged. I don't want Jace to think I'm pressuring him. Not to worry, Jace catches my eye and winks before he slips into the bathroom off the kitchen to change.

I wrap my arms around my momikins. "Well, someone's got to take over your pie empire, and it's not going to be me. What was that loud crash?"

"I dropped a jar on purpose, so you didn't get up to any funny business and miss your surprise." Mom giggles and leans into me. "Now, go on your date night. Lena and I have ten apple pies to make before morning."

"We do need to leave in the next minute or two if we're going to make it." Jace emerges. He's changed into a sweater and dark-black moto jeans. "We have a reservation."

Minutes later, we're heading to some mystery location. I reach over and playfully squeeze his thigh. "C'mon. Where are we going?"

"We haven't had a night out since the band's been on hiatus. I wanted some alone time with my girl." Jace covers my hand with his. "Lena's settled in now. But the past eight months have whizzed by. That trip to Atlanta last spring for Ty's humanitarian award was too short.

Plus, we were subjected to stupid Ty and Zoey drama. I miss having adventures with just you and me."

A lump forms in my throat. "Are you telling me that behind your easygoing cool-guy swagger, you're a romantic at heart?"

"Oh, c'mon. You're questioning my romantic nature?" His expression is mischievous.

He turns onto the Montlake exit and we speed over the floating bridge to the east side. It's kind of glorious being able to chitchat with my guy for a stretch of time with no responsibility. No interruption. I almost forgot what it was like. Time flies by and the next thing I know we're pulling into Marymoor Park. "What are we doing here?"

"It's a surprise." He grins over at me as we park in the VIP section close to a giant blue-and-white tent. He hands me a blindfold. "So, trust me and put this on."

I hold up the scrap of black cloth. "You're serious?"

"I am. Time's a wastin'." He taps his invisible watch.

Obediently, I tie the blindfold around my eyes. I hear Jace get out of the truck and by the crunch of the gravel know he's coming around to my side. My door opens. His strong arms wrap around me to lift me from my seat and place me down gently. He tucks my hand under his bicep and we start walking. He stays noticeably quiet. Without the ability to see, our destination seems like it's taking forever. I don't mind, though, because I'm so excited I can hardly stand it.

I love that Jace is doing this for us.

"We're going up a ramp," Jace whispers. "And stop fidgeting, we're almost there."

Jace leads me inside what I assume is the big tent. We go up some stairs. Then down some more. I smell popcorn. Something sweet. And the smell of barn? I'm so confused but thrilled beyond belief. I love surprises. I love the effort he's put in. He seats me and I feel him sit next to me. When he carefully removes my blindfold, I blink a couple of times and my jaw drops.

We're in the first row, three feet from a circular dirt stage the size of a baseball diamond. A single white horse stands alone in the center. I have no idea what I'm seeing, but I'm blown away. "What is this? Jace?"

He literally beams at me. "It's a show called Cavalia. It's like Cirque du Soleil only with horses. Next weekend is the premiere, but I've arranged for us to watch a private dress rehearsal. Just you and me. Okay?"

"Sooooo okay." I grab his scruffy cheeks and pull him toward me. Give him the hugest kiss.

This is why it's awesome to be in love with a rock star who has all the rock star connections.

Jace slings his arm over my shoulder and the most divine show I'll ever see unfolds before my eyes. Over the course of two hours, dozens of ethereally beautiful horses—in all the colors of the rainbow— take the stage. Sometimes they're on their own. Sometimes they have riders decked out in brilliant costumes. The horses are nearly always surrounded by multicultural dancers, the most stunning visual projections of nature. Not to mention the death-defying acrobats.

It's utterly spectacular.

It's impossible for me to look away. I'm on the edge of my seat. One hand rests on Jace's thigh and I'm pretty sure he'll have fingerprint bruises from how hard I clutch at him every time a new segment starts.

What's most compelling to me personally is how this show treats its horses as the glorious, mythical creatures they truly are. It's so clear they are cherished and loved. It's my perfect night out. A celebration of the horse, my most favorite animal. I'm bawling my eyes out at the spectacle of it all.

When it's over, Jace gets up. Holds his hand out. I take it and someone from the show leads us back to the stables. I lean up and steal a kiss. "I love you so much. This is the best surprise ever."

"No, I love you, Poppy. I knew this show was meant for you." He's walking on air. All because he's pleased me. Gawd. I sometimes wonder how I got so lucky this gorgeous man loves me so much.

We're ushered into a giant holding pen where the horses are being brushed and fed. For the next half hour we're given a behind-the-scenes tour of the inner workings of the show. I'm even able to sneak in sweet snuggles with the amazing animals. Bouncing on my toes, I turn to Jace. "The trainers use Liberty training. I want to learn so bad. Just like on Heartland."

"You and that show." He cracks up at my mention of my favorite Netflix series about a horse ranch in Canada. "I figured this would be inspiring stuff. Good thing I've already arranged for one of their trainers to come out to the ranch to teach us. Lena can learn too."

I throw my arms around my man. "Ohmygod. Are you serious?"

"Dead serious." Jace cups my face with both hands. Kisses me tenderly. "I do have one think to ask you, though."

"Anything. Seriously."

To my complete and total shock, he drops to one knee in front of me. Takes my left hand and brings it to his lips. He's shaking, almost like he's nervous, which can't be true. Jace is the most confident guy in the world. "Poppy, this is long past due. You are everything to me. You'll always be everything to me. I love you more than any words can say. I know I'm not eloquent or sappy. I don't have a sexy Irish accent. But you are mine. I'm yours. It's time to make this official, don't you think? Would you please marry me?"

"Ohmygod. Jace. Yes. Yes. Yes." I kneel down with him and we cling to each other tightly. "Were you scared to ask me?"

"Shitting bricks. All night." He arches an eyebrow and looks down at the ground.

I thread my fingers through his hair. He looks up at me, almost shyly and I absolutely melt. "I've never been the kind of girl who obsesses about a wedding. But Jace? You've got to know, I think you've made me change my mind tonight."

"I didn't know how you'd react. All the guys figured out such grand gestures. I wanted you to have one too." His dimples pop as a smile spreads across his face. "We've gone about things backwards, but I know we're going to have the kind of marriage my parents have. You're it for me."

I'm floored at his sentiment. A little terrified. My parents are divorced. It was ugly, so I've always been a bit skeptical about marriage generally. Which is why I've never, ever wanted to pressure Jace for a ring. Forcing someone to do something they don't want to just isn't...well, me. I must admit, though, with all the LTZ couples being so solid. So in love. Maybe I can accept that Jace and I can make it too.

Besides, we don't need to actually get married.

But hell yeah, of course I want to marry Jace.

One of the performers hands Jace his phone. Leave it to my social-media-expert-now-fiancé to have arranged to capture our special moment. I can't wait to watch it over and over and over. Despite my own insecurities about the marriage thing, I definitely want Jace to feel as special as he's just made me feel. "Babe, this is the most perfect proposal I could have ever hoped for. Seriously. Absolutely blown away."

It's about a thirty-minute drive to the Salish Lodge, where Jace has us booked into a spectacular suite overlooking the 268-foot Snoqualmie Falls waterfall and river. The room is illuminated by dozens of white candles. A tray of chocolate truffles along with Champagne on ice is waiting for us.

When the door shuts behind us, Jace pulls me to him. We melt into each other, kissing, groping, tugging our clothes off as fast as possible. He cups my ass and yanks me against his thick cock. "We have whole a night of uninterrupted naked-time, are you ready?"

"Gawd, yes."

We make love until dawn. Like we used to do all those years ago when we were sneaking around Europe together. When we truly fell in love.

Back then, I wasn't ready for him. I was too afraid Jace would eventually break my heart.

Tonight? It's so clear.

He's mine. The future is finally ours, and I'm diving in headfirst.

48

Chapter Four

Three Weeks Later

I'M NOT QUITE SURE if I've been dreading this meeting or looking forward to it. Truth be told, I've been so focused on my girls, I haven't been behind my drum kit for months. Haven't thought about touring. Or writing. Or playing.

In the weeks since Alex and I got engaged, our folks have hounded us to get a date on the books.

As for the two of us? We haven't talked about it once. Which is why I'm leaning toward Vegas. Alex and I aren't big planners. We're doers. That would be a surefire way to make her Mrs. Deveraux.

"Dude, it's good to see you." Ty embraces me when he and I step through the front door to his house in West Seattle. "Connor and Zane aren't here yet. Zoey told me you and Alex got engaged. Congratulations. Sounded pretty epic."

I follow him into the kitchen where he hands me a bottle of water. "Thanks, my brother. It was a long time coming. I got the low-down on your trip from Alex. Sounds like your time away was pretty epic too."

"Yeah. It's about time I got a little taste of what you guys had all of those years." Ty's smile doesn't quite reach his eyes. He looks out the window and his eyebrows squinch together for a couple of minutes before he focuses back on me with a genuine expression of happiness. "Having time with just me and Zoey was really, really great."

Before I can help myself, I slip into my old caretaking pattern. "You okay?"

"Yeah, of course. You don't need to worry about me anymore, Jace. Seriously." Ty pulls me into a hug.

Things are still just a slight bit raw between me and our singer since my outburst at his engagement party last Christmas Eve. I said some truthful, but hurtful shit. He's a sensitive soul. Considering we're heading into the holidays soon, I don't want there to be any weirdness anymore. I thunk his back with my fist before stepping back. "I'm still here for you, Ty. I know I apologized for my behavior at your engagement party, but I'm sorry I haven't been around. It's just...I needed a little break from everything."

"I appreciate that. I do. No need to apologize. I'm the one who's terribly sorry for all the drama Zoey and I have caused. And for all you had to take on. I'm locked down now though. I promise. Especially now that Zoey and I are getting married."

Thank gawd.

The doorbell rings but I want to close out the conversation. "All that past shit is behind us. Yeah?"

"Yeah." Ty nods as he walks backward toward the door. "For sure."

Seconds later, Zane and Connor bound into the kitchen. Ty leads us downstairs to his newly renovated home studio. It's a sound-tech's dream setup. The thing is? As cool as the state-of-the-art equipment is, I'm not inspired to record new songs. I hope everyone feels the way I do. I need a bit of time before we get back to band business.

Either way, I'll go with the flow. After all, LTZ is a democracy.

Despite my reticence at getting back to work, I can't help but feel a certain level of comfort at hanging with the guys I've been in the trenches with for years. "The studio turned out awesome. Maybe, when we're ready, we should just record the next stuff here." I move over to the mixing board and run my fingers along the knobs. "You have enough guest rooms; we could all just stay with you."

Ty looks horrified. We all laugh and assure him it's a joke. Then we make small talk about what we've been up to.

Connor seems tense. He's participating but keeps glancing at his phone. After twenty minutes or so he clearly wants us to get to the point of our visit. "My dudes, please. Let's get down to business. Da's going in for his procedure tomorrow, so I gotta get back home." He motions for everyone to sit.

"My brothers, I'm just going to keep it simple. I need more time. I hope you understand." Ty shocks the life out of me when he practically pulls the words from my head.

"Thank God." Zane pinches the bridge of his nose. "Fee is buried with everything that needs to get done for the restaurant opening. We still need time to dial it all in."

I'm quick to agree. "I'm cool with that."

Connor lets out a sigh of relief. "Aye. That's grand. The thought of going back out on the road right now? Feck no. But I do miss writing and recording. And playing, if I'm honest. I want to come up with a plan so the kids can be with us. One that lets us take long breaks. Many long breaks. I don't ever want to be gone for years at a time again."

I'm so relieved I can barely stand it. The thought of being without Alex and Lena is inconceivable. Now that I know my band's on the same page, it's like a huge weight has been lifted. The energy in the room is certainly lighter, and we're all able to relax and banter for a while.

"Guys, Zoey and I are getting married sometime in the next couple of weeks," Ty makes an announcement I figured was coming. "We just decided to go for it this morning, so I don't have the exact date. It won't be a big wedding. Just her family. Carter. All of us. The girls. The kids. I think that's it."

As Ty speaks and the guys congratulate him, a vision of Alex twirling around in a flirty little white gown wearing a crown of daisies permeates my mind. Goddammit. Our timing is usurped by Ty and Zoey.

Again.

I'm happy for them, but it's hard not to feel just a slight bit annoyed at myself for waiting so long to make things official with Alex.

"Before we set the date, I wanted to check in with all of you to figure out what's most convenient for everyone." Ty's puppy-dog eyes make it impossible to be anything but happy for him. He's so fucking earnest. All the time.

"Dude, whatever day you pick, we'll be there. Text me when and where." Connor heads upstairs. "Seriously. Congratulations. I'm sorry but I gotta jet. Duty calls."

The three of us follow him up. After he leaves, we convene in the kitchen, where Ty offers to cook. "Sooooo...." Zane slings an arm around my shoulder. "Double wedding? Alex and you. Ty and Zoey. Perfect, right?"

"Uh." I glance around the room. Alex would hate taking away from Zoey's special day. "Nah."

Ty pulls out a container of fresh Dungeness crab and a bunch of ingredients from his crazy-huge commercial refrigerator. "I'm sure Zoey wouldn't care. I mean if we're all in town." He shrugs.

"See!" Zane claps me on the back. "Married life is awesome. Join us. Join us." He waggles his fingers at me like he's casting a magic spell.

"I don't think a double wedding's the way to go for us." I tap out a rhythm on the counter. "Maybe we'll just elope."

Ty warms up the crab mixture he's just put together. "You'll be at our wedding though?"

"Of course, dude. I wouldn't miss it," I assure him.

"Why would you elope? We hated missing Connor's wedding." Zane scrunches up his nose.

I'm getting a little exasperated at being put on the spot when Alex and I haven't talked about what we're going to do.

"Uh, Jace? You there?" Zane waves his hand two inches from my eyes.

"It's just an idea. Let me work out the details with Poppy and you guys will be first to know." I decide to change the subject. "How's the restaurant coming? Is Fiona close to opening?"

"Fuck, no." Zane sighs heavily. "Between contractors bailing on us and failed inspections, it's been a nightmare. Neither of us have any experience with construction. Luckily, Connor's brother is on the job now. We should have brought McLoughlin Construction in from the very beginning."

Ty places the most delectable buttery crab rolls on the placemats. "Here you go."

"Fuuuuck. Ty. Be warned, Fiona's threatening to recruit you. She's having a hell of a time staffing up." Zane shakes his head and closes his eyes. "These are orgasmic."

I lick sauce off my fingers and tease our singer. "You could just wear a wig. No one will recognize you. We all have some time on our hands now."

Ty rolls his eyes and stops to take a call from Zoey. We retreat into the living room to continue catching up until she gets home. The minute Zoey unlocks the door,

Ty swoops over to her and shoves his tongue down her throat. PDAs have always been their MO.

"Jesus," I can't help but scoff. "You two never stop."

Zoey's narrowed eyes catch mine and she wags her finger at me. "Are you being serious right now? Last time I was over at your house I literally caught you going down on my best friend in the horse barn. I'll never unsee that."

Ah. True that. All I can do is shrug. Luckily, I'm saved by my phone buzzing in my pocket. "Poppy, I'm still at Ty and Zoey's, you're on speaker. Say hello."

"Hey, everyone." Alex's jubilant voice permeates the room. "Send my man home, will you? I need his help for our expanding family. Oh, and Zoey? We're making a date for you to come over. No excuses."

"Yes, ma'am," Zoey answers in a singsong voice. "Remember I'm meeting you for lunch downtown after your appointment next week."

Of course, Ty is clueless. "Holy shit! Is Alex pregnant?"

"Fuck no," I snarl at him and can't help but laugh at our perpetually distracted singer. "We just added two new horses to the ranch. Do you ever listen to anything I say?"

Ty winces but recovers in an instant. Zane comes to his rescue, as always. You'd think they were real brothers.

"Don't sweat it. You zoned out earlier when he told us the story."

Zoey snuggles up to him and brushes the hair from his eyes. He gazes at her adoringly. I take this as my cue to head out. As much as the reunion with my bandmates was needed, I'd much rather be with my own family. "Welp, I've got to head out to catch the ferry." I get up and say my goodbyes.

On my drive to catch the boat back to the island, I call Alex. "Good news. LTZ is taking time off. Oh, and Ty and Zoey are getting married in the next couple of weeks."

"I already knew about the wedding, silly." Alex sounds out of breath. "So, not to cut you off but Lena's down for a nap. Can I just see you at home? I have a miniscule window of opportunity to straighten up the house."

I can't help but laugh. "Are you wearing your French maid uniform?"

"Ohmygawd." She snorts. "Get off that train of thought. Never. Going. To. Happen."

"You're a sucker for costumes. It will happen, Poppy," I say with confidence.

Alex laughs. "You're probably right. I'm a sucker for a costume. Get your ass home. Stat."

I chill out on the ferry ride home feeling great about the day. My band brothers mean the world to me. They do. But my life with Alex and Lena is most important right now. I'm going to protect our family bubble for as long as possible.

Now that we're officially engaged, a little part of me deep, deep inside carries some hope we'll have more kids. She'd always been against the idea until Lena though, so I won't push her. We're still young. She and I have plenty of time to figure it out.

Whether or not she's willing to expand our family, I'm not going to take her or Lena for granted. Ever.

They're truly all I need.

It's hard to believe how perfect our life is.

I'm going to do everything in my power to keep it this way.

Chapter Five

IT'S FUNNY HOW THINGS have changed between me and Zoey but have also stayed status quo.

My BFF is finally back from traveling the world with her fiancé. It's been a little over seven months since we've had an in-depth heart-to-heart. Sure, she texted me and sent pictures every now and then, but nothing substantive since we were all in Atlanta at an awards banquet where Ty was honored for his charity. While he was on stage accepting his trophy, I ended up taking care of her in the VIP bathroom.

And then, the next day, she and Ty were gone.

Oh, I'm cool with it. We can go for months without talking. For instance, after she broke things off with Ty before LTZ went on their first tour, she lost touch with everyone but her parents. She essentially dropped off the planet. I put in a bit of effort, but after a while, I stopped reaching out.

Not because I was mad. I wasn't. We've been like sisters ever since we were little kids. Our friendship is unbreakable.

Plus, I was secretly hooking up with Ty's bandmate and didn't tell her. Neither of us is perfect.

In any case, every girl should have a Zoey in her life. Someone who will be loyal until the day you die and, when it matters, show up for you. So, yeah. I'm glad she's back. A girl needs her best friend.

I would love to talk to her about what's happening with me. Get a woman's perspective. The thing is? I'm terrified. My cramps are getting worse. And worse. And worse. My usual ways of managing my pain aren't working so Jace used his rock-star connections to schedule an appointment with a specialist.

He friggin' watched over my shoulder as I did it.

Before the specialist would see me, I had to visit my regular doctor for a referral. Stupid health insurance. Luckily, the timing worked out perfectly since I was already coming into the city to lunch with Zoey. I've already been poked and prodded and ultrasounded by the time I pull into her driveway. I barely kill the engine before Zoey bursts through her front door. "Hey!" She flings herself into my arms. "I've missed you so much."

I resist bursting into tears. "I've missed you so much. I was bummed when you couldn't make it out this weekend, so I decided to come to you."

"I'm sorry I'm such a sucky friend." Zoey is so serious, which cracks me up. "I just have so much to do for the wedding."

"I was kidding, butterfly." I use Ty's nickname for her to let her know I'm not actually mad at her.

Her relief is evident when she jumps in the car. I drive to Alki Beach to have lunch at Duke's Chowder House. To me, nothing screams Seattle more than eating a bowl of delicious clam chowder and gazing out at Puget Sound. We take a seat at the window. Order our food and clasp hands across the table.

"So, are you pregnant yet?" I tease.

Zoey rests her chin on her hand and stares at me dreamily. "Not yet. Hopefully soon. I've only been off birth control for a couple of weeks."

"What? What does that mean? You're not at least using condoms?" I'm blown away. Sure, they're engaged, but they've been back together for a year. A lot of that time has been tumultuous. I want to tell her that jumping into parenthood too fast can be challenging, but I don't. It's not for me to tell her what to do. Or what not to do, as the case may be.

She laughs, somewhat nervously. "Nope. We decided to just let nature take its course. Both of us want to start our family."

"Holy shit." I bring my hands up to my cheeks and bug my eyes out dramatically like that kid from Home Alone.

Zoey looks like she desperately wants to say something else, but she doesn't. Instead looks down at her chowder, stirring oyster crackers around. "I just hope we're ready. Ty says he is. And I think I am?"

"Have the headaches gone away?" I'm dying to know because of what I'm going through. "My doctor is running a battery of tests. I wonder if my cramps are a hormonal thing too."

"Jace's wonder-tongue isn't making it all better?" Zoey never can resist reminding me that she caught Jace going down on me in the barn earlier this year. I mean, it wasn't my fault she took the earlier ferry that day. My cramps were bad, as usual. Jace and I thought we had another hour before she got there.

I hold up my hand. "Argh. I can't believe you caught us like that. Ewww."

"Oh, but I did." She waggles her eyebrows.

"Well, I can't believe I confided in you that he calls oral sex 'the cure.' It totally helps with the cramps, though." I shoot her the evil eye.

"If he's anything like Ty, I'm sure going down on you isn't a hardship for him."

"Yeah. I guess we're lucky our rock stars are both down with the swirl."

We giggle profusely.

"So, are you still loving being a mom?" She gazes dreamily at me.

"I am." My eyes unexpectedly moisten for the second time today. "Lena is truly the light of my life."

Zoey swoons. "See? That's what I want too. I'm a little jealous of you guys. I want to have a baby so bad. Then our kids can grow up together."

The thought warms my heart. "That would be so cool. But you did say you hope you're ready. Just remember, it's not easy." I dunk a piece of buttered sourdough bread into the creamy chowder and savor.

"Well..." She wrinkles her nose. "Here's what I keep coming back to. Are you ever ready? We have some things to work out, but we'll get there."

"You don't sound convinced." I scrutinize her expression. Even though Ty's a great guy and they are soulmates and everything, they've had so much drama in their relationship. As the band's de facto social media guy, Jace has spent hundreds of hours trying to deal with it. I know how much he's over it.

She looks out the window and then back at me with conviction. "No, I am completely convinced. Ty and I are solid. We're not the same immature kids anymore. The wedding is happening. So's a baby. Right now? I'm so incredibly happy you're going to be my maid of honor."

"I'd kill you if it wasn't me, you realize," I joke, but I'm shocked when an emotion I'm not used to washes over me. Envy. Jace and I might be engaged, but I've been reluctant to set a date. It freaks me out a bit. "What do you need me to do?"

She shrugs. "Not much. It's such a tiny wedding. Only the band, us gals, the kids, and my folks. Maybe Carter. And your mom if she's free. Maybe you could help me pick out my dress and some bridesmaid dresses next weekend?"

"Done." We grip each other's hands and squeal for a second.

Zoey and I spend the rest of the afternoon chatting about her world travels. My challenges trying to get through my certification program for horse therapy. Connor and Ronni's adorable infant twin sons. Fiona's restaurant. The future of LTZ. All in all, the perfect afternoon.

By the time we've exhausted our conversation, it's dark outside and my cramps are back in full force. When we stand to go, I double over in pain and plop back down. Rummage through my bag to find the 222s. "Gawd, I'm so sick of this. I can't wait to find out what the doctor thinks is going on."

"I'm so glad you're not ignoring this anymore, Alex. Better to be safe than sorry." Zoey helps me to the car. "Trust me, it feels empowering to take control of the situation."

"Yeah." A quick pang of fear roils in my gut, but I tamp it down. I'm in the best shape of my life. Jace and I eat super healthy. We're active. Bad cramps are likely just hereditary. My mom's lived with it her whole life. And my sister. It's not going to be anything serious. How could it be?

We say our goodbyes and by the time I pick up Lena, catch the ferry back and get home, I'm exhausted, but at least the medication has kicked in.

"There's my girls," Jace greets us at the door and takes Lena. "I missed you."

After he puts her to bed, he joins me on the porch where I'm waiting with a couple glasses of Catherine Syrah from XOBC Cellars. We clink our glasses together. "So, they're trying for a baby."

"Oh?" Jace keeps his voice neutral.

"Yeah."

He digs his thumbs into my soles. "I'm glad. It will be nice for Lena to have other kids around. Connor suggested that when we start touring again, we make it family friendly and bring the kids. A lot of bands do it, I think it's a great idea."

We sit in silence for a bit as he works on my foot massage.

"After we're married, should we be thinking about giving Lena a sibling?" I say it so quietly I'm not sure if Jace hears me. The topic of having our own children is always a bit, well, delicate. Because of me and my past stance on not wanting kids. A little part of me wonders if that's the reason why it took so long for Jace to propose. After my day with Zoey and her excitement about getting pregnant, I can't help asking.

Jace keeps working on my foot. His voice is equally quiet. Unsure. "Are you saying you want to have a baby?"

"I know I was adamant...before." I let the admission hang in the air.

His mouth sets in a grim line. He shuts his eyes and sighs. "Are we able to talk about it without getting our feelings hurt?"

"I hope so. I thought once we adopted Lena you'd realize... But I guess we've never had a conversation about having our own children."

He drops my feet and sits on the edge of the swing. Scrubs his hands through his hair. "I didn't realize there was a conversation to be had. I told you I want to be with you more than having kids. Adopting Lena is enough..."

"Is it?" I grab his hand to interrupt him. "I mean because I think I do. Want to have a baby, that is."

He looks over at me, skeptically. "You're not just saying that?"

I play with his fingers. They've always been a bit calloused because of his drumming. Now, they're rugged because of all the work he does around the ranch. "I was young. Immature. Scarred from my parents' divorce and how long it took for me to forgive my dad. Back then, I wasn't sure that you actually wanted to be with me. I just...things are not even remotely like before. We're engaged. We already have one kid..."

"You said after we get married. Do you want to set a wedding date? You haven't brought it up since we got engaged." He sucks in a breath of air.

I'm genuinely confused because I was thinking the exact thing. "What do you mean?"

"Let's go to Vegas. This weekend. We can even bring Lena." He stands and walks to the edge of the porch. Looks out toward the stable.

In a flash, I'm by his side. "Are you being serious?"

"What if I am? I just want us to be married." He shrugs.

I'm shocked, though. "But Vegas? Really?"

"Yeah…" He drags his answer out like a question.

I hate the idea with a passion. I can't believe that's how he wants our wedding to go down after his epic proposal. So, I deflect. And fib. Like an asshole. "If you don't want to have a real wedding, you know there's no pressure from me. We're already married in spirit."

He grips my shoulders and peers down at me. "You said that before I proposed. Tell me. What does 'married in spirit' even mean?"

"Uhhh." I have no answer. It seemed like a cool, nonchalant thing to say, though.

"Oh-kay. So, could you give me some indication as to what kind of wedding you want? It doesn't matter to me. We can get married on horseback here at the ranch. Fly to some exotic location like Zane and Fiona. Elope like

Connor and Ronni. If you tell me what kind of wedding you dream about, I'll make it happen."

"My gawd, you are such a closet romantic." When I make a move to pull away, the stupid cramps take my breath and the topic of a wedding is forgotten. I can't help but wince and plop back down on the porch swing.

"You're still hurting?" He scans my body. "Should I try the cure?"

"I don't think it's going to work. They're so bad today."

He holds out his hand. "C'mon. Lena's fast asleep. I'll at least give it a try."

Jace leads me into the bedroom. We kneel on the bed. He strips off the blue-checked plaid shirt I'm wearing, which is actually his. His thumbs stroke my collarbone and jawline. "I love you." He nuzzles my cheek as he unfastens my white bralette.

"I love you too." I smooth his hair from his face. Our lips meet. Tongues tangle. It's sweet. It's gentle. A stabbing pain slices through my lower belly causing me to crumple to the bed.

"Poppy, I hate seeing you like this so much." His face is scrunched up with worry.

I'm in the fetal position, my knees nearly touching my chin. "Please. Please try to make it go away."

Jace unfurls my legs to pull down my jeans and panties. He settles between my legs and savors me. Takes his sweet, sweet time. Wiggles his tongue on my clit. Inserts one, then two fingers inside me. Every muscle in my body feels atrophied from bearing the intense pain. When the pleasure begins to register it's like waves of warm water allow my limbs to loosen. Replaced with delicious, sparky, shivering sensations making me forget about the cramps.

"That's it," he murmurs against my lower lips when my legs fall slack against the sheets. Then he goes to town. Jace's skills at eating me out have been honed to perfection. He knows exactly when to lick and exactly when to suck to drive me to oblivion. Soon, I'm lazily thrusting against his mouth while he curls his fingers inside me and rubs my G-spot hard.

I clutch the sheets on either side of his head, writhing from the ecstasy. The buildup of the impending orgasm blessedly pushes the pain away. I begin chanting, "Oh gawd. Oh sweet gawd," when Jace presses his tongue against my clit and swirls. Hard. Harder. Holy fucking shit. I'm annihilated by the orgasm. It's so powerful, my entire body quakes.

Seconds later, Jace drives into me. One knee shoved under my thigh, which he holds open with his palm. We're a grinding, slapping, bucking whirlwind, until I'm convulsing from another powerful release. Abruptly, he pulls out and flips me on my stomach and pulls my hips up. Slams into me from behind. He fingers my clit and angles himself so his dick hits my hidden spot. Relentlessly. My entire body explodes with pleasure again. And again.

"I fucking love you," Jace moans as he gushes inside me moments later. We collapse on the bed, a panting, sweaty mess.

It's hard not to smile.

There's nothing to worry about, Jace and I are married in spirit, whatever that means...

Everything between us is perfect as it is.

Chapter Six

Three Weeks Later

ALEX DOESN'T THINK I can hear her crying.

When she's hurting, it kills me. Physical pain is one thing. Mental pain is even worse. Especially because she's so fucking strong. Independent. Able to handle anything. Just not when she has these fucking cramps. They happen all the time now.

She's utterly helpless.

Years ago, I knew she suffered a little bit. Back then, she and I were hooking up all over Europe when LTZ was on tour. I didn't think about it too deeply because, well, I'm a dude. My band was getting famous. I was busy running LTZ's social media. What did I know about a woman's cycle? My sisters sure never shared anything about that subject matter with me.

It wasn't until I moved to the ranch when I realized just how much pain she truly tolerated.

I couldn't stand it. Still can't. I'm a fixer, so I wanted to find a solution even though she assured me her pain was normal. Faced with long stretches of time on the bus, I started researching. I came across an article about how orgasms helped stop a woman's cramps. It became my mission to compile the best-of-the-best techniques to make sure Alex came so hard her cramps would go away.

That's how it started. When I was in Hong Kong, we played a festival with a band called 22 Goats. Somehow, I got into a conversation about female orgasms with their singer, Dax Morgan and his wife, Violet. They gleefully shared a technique that has been life-changing. For both me and Alex.

Ever since, when we have some time—at least a couple of hours preferably—and privacy, I take matters into my own hands—and well, lips and tongue and fingers—and it works spectacularly. First, I make sure she's fully relaxed and then I take my sweet time to make her come over and over again until she's a satisfied noodle. Then, and only then, I fuck her senseless until we both explode and Jesus... It's goddamn nirvana. For both of us.

There's something fucking life changing when you orgasm after a long-delayed gratification. Just sayin'.

These days, I'm in a constant state of delayed gratification. It's difficult to fit quick sex in. We're lucky if we manage a couple times a week. Let alone a fuckathon. I've fallen down on the job, and I feel guilty. Yesterday, Poppy couldn't even get out of bed. She laid under the covers in a fetal position all day. I felt so helpless.

A double dose of her beloved 222s didn't make a dent in the pain so I called Alex's regular doctor to get a prescription for stronger pain meds. I'm hoping it holds her over until her appointment with the specialist.

I rap lightly on the bathroom door. "Hey, can I come in?"

"Can you give me a sec?" She clears her throat. "I'll be okay. I took the pill. But I'm not happy about it. Prescription drugs are not a long-term solution."

"I know, but it was an emergency, Poppy. We don't have to go to the wedding. Seriously." I know Ty and Zoey will be upset, but Alex's health is more important.

She bursts through the door; tears stain her cheeks. "I'm not missing my best friend's wedding. No way."

"I love you." I wrap her snugly against my chest and caress her back. "When you're hurting like this, you have to understand, all I want to do is take it all away. I'd do anything to swap places."

Her body shakes. Her fingers flex and grip my shoulders. "I hate being such a burden."

"You are never a burden." I cup her cheeks and stroke her lips with my thumb. "We're in this together. We're going to figure it out."

"I'm counting the days until we meet with Dr. Madison in person." Alex is so incredibly vulnerable at the moment, a characteristic she rarely lets anyone see. I'll never take it for granted that she trusts me enough to show this side of herself.

I press my finger to her lips then tuck her hair behind her ears. "Shh. One thing at a time. Lena's down for her nap. All our stuff for the wedding is in the truck. We can take a minute to rest and regroup before we have to catch the ferry."

Alex allows me to lead her out to the porch where we cuddle on our porch swing. It's our spot. She tucks her long, pajama-clad legs up to her chest and rests her head on my lap. My palm spans her head so my thumbs can lightly circle her temple. After a few minutes she lets out a huge breath and her entire body relaxes. I sink back into the swing and let out a breath when her breathing evens out.

Gawd, I wish I could take away her pain.

As the time ticks by, my body aches from remaining essentially frozen in position but I'm afraid to move. The last thing I want to do is disturb her. She hasn't slept well in three days. I want her to rest as long as possible. Soon, we'll all be at Ty and Zoey's house for their wedding. I just want her to have a few moments of peace before she does what she always does—push her needs aside to give her all to her bestie.

I hope Zoey appreciates it.

She gets a little over an hour of sleep before I hear Lena babbling at Mitch through the baby monitor and have no choice but to move. "Alex, Lena's up. If we're going to make the wedding, we need to get going," I lean down and whisper into her ear.

"Mmm." She nods without opening her eyes. I gently move her into a sitting position. Yawning, Alex raises her arms high above her head and stretches, shaking her wrists to wake herself up. "Huh. I feel okay. I actually feel normal."

We both go to Lena's room. I change her diaper while Alex steams her flower girl dress. After I throw her stinky poo-filled diaper in the genie, I ask, "When do we start potty training again?"

"Soon. Probably a month or so after the new year. Her pediatrician told me if we start too early it will take longer for her to learn." Alex pinches her nose with her fingers. "That's a bad one. What did you feed her?"

"Uh, bananas. Ground chicken. Cheese." Talking about baby poop. That's what we're reduced to now. It's crazy how much our life has changed. Aside from Alex's cramp situation, I wouldn't trade my new life one bit.

Alex takes Lena from me and boops her nose. "Well, aren't you the smelly one? No cheese and bananas combo for you, missy. Are you ready to see auntie Zoey get married to Uncle Ty?"

"Yah. I flowa girl." Lena giggles. "Me see Mia."

"Yes, you'll see your cousin Mia and your new baby cousins Toran and Tristan." She twirls our daughter around. "And your rocker uncles and aunties. Today's going to be incredibly fun."

It nearly brings a tear to my eye to see Alex laughing with Lena after how bad she felt not long ago. These little moments, I tell you. They're everything. I gather my girls and we head out.

⁓

The wedding, of course, is touching and surprisingly low key. It's clear that Ty and Zoey are blissfully happy. I'm stoked that all of the drama we've lived through for the past decade is behind us. Even if it weren't, I'd be done with it because I've got much more important priorities now. Managing Ty's emotions isn't at the top of my list anymore.

It's not on any list at all.

Connor sidles up to me with one of his boys. "It's good they're getting their happily ever after, isn't it?"

"Yep." I nod.

"You're not still salty, are you?" He purses his lips.

"Nah. I'm just over it. I love Ty. I love Zoey. I just want off the crazy train." I glance over at Alex and Zoey, who are dancing with Lena and Mia, Zane and Fiona's daughter. Ty's talking with Carter, Zane's dad, and Zoey's parents. "I really just want to focus on my own family."

"About that..." He doesn't finish his sentence. Just stares at me. A pointed gaze from our bass player is usually all it takes to get his point across.

I shrug. "Life is good."

"Feckin' hell." He rolls his eyes. "Ronni said you got engaged. Were you thinking of telling me?"

"Uh, I guess so?"

"Dude." His eyes bore into mine. He shifts his son to his other arm. Says nothing else.

"What?"

"When's the wedding? You're the last man standing." He shakes his head like I'm an idiot.

Alex and I still haven't picked up the conversation. We've been too focused on her health. "We're married in spirit. Don't rush us. It will happen. We haven't set a date yet."

"What the hell does that even mean?" Connor squeezes his eyes shut and shakes his head like I'm an annoying little brother.

"Dunno. We'll figure it out."

Ronni appears at Connor's side with their other twin. "Don't pressure him, babe. That's not cool."

"Thank you, Ronni." I squeeze her to my side. "You're the voice of reason."

"Aye, that she is." Connor kisses his wife and gazes at her with reverence. "Plus, she found an innovative artist management company we can check out. If we're really going to make the switch, that is."

"Hmm." I say noncommittally. After all, we still have a couple months off before we go back to work. Nothing needs to get decided yet. We don't need to make any big moves.

Zane and Fiona join us. "What's this I hear about you being engaged?" Zane pouts.

"Jesus. It's not like it's big news. I proposed weeks ago. We live together. We have a daughter. No big deal." I throw up my arms in indignation.

Fee crosses her arms and scolds, "Stop it with the cool-guy stuff, Jace. At least you put a ring on it, we're all thrilled you finally got your shit together."

I must look annoyed because Zane, ever the peacemaker, says gently, "Fee, we need to lay off. It's their business."

"Alex is the best, though." Fee's liquid-aqua eyes narrow. "I want her to be happy."

Fear pierces my heart, which leads me to uncharacteristically overshare. "Did she say something to you? Because she's the one who won't set the date, not me."

"She's dealing with some health stuff, Fee." Ronni touches her arm.

"Oh, God." Fiona's eyes widen with horror.

Now all eyes are on me just as Alex walks up with Lena in her arms. "What's going on?"

"I'm not sure." I feel utterly and totally exposed. Alex and I do not air our business to people. I mean, she talks to Zoey of course, but I have literally no idea what Fee and Ronni know, or what Alex has confided in them about her upcoming doctor visit.

"Are you okay, honey?" Fiona tentatively touches Alex's shoulder.

Alex's eyes catch mine. "Um, yeah?"

"I think I said something I shouldn't have." Ronni winces. "I didn't know you were keeping the situation private. I'm so sorry."

Now I'm confused. "What situation is that?"

Alex grips my wrist. "All of the girls were talking about my doctor visit this week. Fee, to catch you up, I'm having abnormal cramping and Jace and I are going to a specialist so I can hopefully get to the bottom of it this week." She's talking to the group but looking at me. "Basically, we're both tired of playing Internet doctor. It's scary out there."

I suck in a breath. It's kinda freaking me out that she's sharing our private business with our friends. Growing up with a father whose moves were scrutinized at every turn, I learned to keep my family shit tight. I'm not going to make a scene here at the wedding, however. "I didn't realize we were sharing yet, Poppy." I wince before I can control my reaction.

"C'mon Jace. Lighten up. Female-related health issues have been a taboo subject for too long," Ronni scolds. "It's important we share these experiences. Keeping things like this secret is not okay. Did you know that the percentage of money spent on research into women's reproductive health is astonishingly low? You have a daughter. Think about it."

Zane's and Connor's expressions are priceless. Utter and total discomfort. Connor has a weird smile pasted on his face. Zane's looking around the room for an escape route. Fee high-fives Ronni.

As for me, I feel a bit attacked because I know these statistics. I've done my research. It's just that...Alex's situation is personal to us. I'm frustrated that everyone seems to now know our business when we really aren't entirely sure what's up yet.

I'm about to speak up when Alex rests her head on my arm and loops her hand around my elbow. "Jace isn't the bad guy here, Ronni. He's done more to help me than I've done to help myself. While I appreciate what you're saying, we'll make the best decision for ourselves. I'm happy to share what's going on, but our solution is not up for group discussion or debate."

Mic drop. Courtesy: my badass fairy ninja.

"Maybe let's lighten the mood and play some music?" Zane asks hopefully.

Connor nods enthusiastically. "Aye. Let's."

So, we manage to spend the rest of Ty and Zoey's wedding as it should be.

Full of love. Laughter. Family. Music, of course.

After witnessing her ability to not only diffuse the uncomfortable situation but defend me in the process, I realize now, more than ever, Alex is so completely and utterly perfect just the way she is. I'll do anything to keep her safe. Healthy.

As far as our wedding goes? Yeah, well. I'm going to convince Alex to pick a path after we figure out what's wrong.

Because once we get this thing resolved, everything will fall back into place.

Of that, I've never been more certain.

Chapter Seven

Two Weeks Later

THIS IS SERIOUSLY THE last place on earth I want to be today.

I try to concentrate on my reward. Lena's first Christmas season. After I'm done, we're taking Lena to visit Santa. Lunch at The Metropolitan Grill. A nap in our room at the Four Seasons. Later, the tree-lighting ceremony at Macy's complete with carousel ride and treats.

It's also our first Christmas as a family, after all. I want it to be special. Create our own traditions.

For now, she's with my mom while I wait to get poked and prodded again by my new specialist. Hopefully, I can get to the bottom of this bullshit pain and rid myself of it forever.

"You tired?" Jace takes my hand and places it on his thigh when I rest my head on his shoulder.

"Uh, yeah. I appreciate you getting us a private appointment so no one else is here, but did we have to be here at seven in the morning?" I yawn, making a point of whooshing out a big gust of breath.

Jace kisses the top of my head. "Uh, yeah. I did. It's not like you're not already up at this time of the morning on a normal day."

A nurse appears at the door. "Ms. LeRoux? Dr. Madison is ready."

Jace and I stand. He keeps a tight hold on my hand. Squeezes. I look up into his handsome face. His long hair is tucked into a beanie. His green eyes bore into mine with the most devastatingly concerned look. His lips curl into an encouraging smile, causing his dimples to pop out beneath a day's worth of stubble. God, how I love him. He's all quiet strength and comfort. Effortless cool which comes from within.

I need him. So badly.

There's no one on earth who makes me feel safer. It's taken a lot for me to embrace how much I rely on him.

"My fiancé is coming too," I say to the nurse as I squeeze his hand back. "This affects us both."

Once we're in the examining room, Dr. Madison motions for us to sit. To my surprise, she wastes little time. "Alex, I'm sure you're frustrated by not having any clear diagnosis or treatment plan. Prescriptions for strong pain killers are not the long-term answer. You're a young mother, no need to contribute to the opioid crisis if we don't have to."

My jaw drops. She's so on point, I can't even speak.

"My suspicion is that you have endometriosis." She leans over and rests her forearms on her knees so she can look me directly in the eye. "Too many times my patients tell me when they've complained about the pain, their mother, friends, partners, and even their physicians, say, 'periods are supposed to hurt, that's normal' and they don't do anything. They grin and bear it. Endure being a female if you will. Unfortunately, no one seems to take it seriously until things get really bad."

Jace turns to me. "Huh. Poppy, for years, you've said your cramps are normal."

"Well, that's what every gyno I've ever seen has told me." I shrug. "How would I know any different?"

"So, what is endometriosis?" He stares intently at the doctors. "How do we cure it?"

She brushes invisible lint from her sleeve. "Well, in a nutshell, it's a condition where tissue similar to the tissue in a woman's uterine lining grows outside the uterus. It reacts the same way too. It can shed. And bleed. Symptoms range from nothing at all to severe pain. It can be mild or invasive. Unfortunately, there are still quite a few unknowns."

"I don't understand." I'm shocked that no one thought to tell me this. Or that I didn't even consider this possibility with all my Internet research. "Why am I just learning about this now?"

Dr. Madison leans back in her chair. "Endometriosis is difficult to diagnose, mainly because it's not easy to see or feel using traditional tools or techniques such as a pelvic exam and ultrasounds. For many women, they aren't able to have any answers without laparoscopy. It's a fairly noninvasive surgical procedure where a woman's internal organs are examined for deep endometriosis implants, ovarian cysts, and scar tissue."

"Wait, so Alex has to have surgery?" Jace grips my knee.

"Maybe not. Your primary care physician referred you to me because I specialize in an innovative technique." Dr. Madison points to a cart with what appears to be a laptop sitting on top connected to a bunch of fancy gadgets. "I've been using this special ultrasound machine to obtain super-high-quality images of my patients' reproductive organs. I'm able to see everything in 3D, which potentially allows me to get your condition diagnosed expeditiously and accurately. Then, we can come up with a treatment plan."

I scrutinize the machine. "So, you'll be able to figure out what's going on today? Gawd. I don't know what I thought would happen today, but this is not what I had in mind."

"Potentially. With the ultrasound, we've been able to see what we're dealing with, measure endometrial thickness reliably, hopefully to eliminate exploratory surgery." Dr. Madison wheels the machine closer to us. "This little beauty saves time and is incredibly accurate. Not to mention it's much less invasive."

Ten minutes later, Jace and I stare into the monitor as Dr. Madison slides the smooth sensor over every inch of my abdomen, stopping to take pictures now and then. I don't dare speak because it's so abundantly clear my insides are a mess.

When she's finished, and I'm cleaned up, he and I resume our previous positions in the chairs across from her desk. She hands us a couple of pictures of my innards and points to the areas where what looks like sea sponges coat parts of my reproductive organs. "Alex, it appears to me that you have deep, infiltrating endometriosis." She points to two particularly blobby-looking patches "Here and here indicate the presence of what we call 'chocolate cysts,' which are usually benign, but we will want to take samples to be sure."

Throughout all of this discussion, I haven't been able to look at Jace. It's hard not to be horrified by what's growing inside my body, I can't imagine how he feels. When I venture a peek, I see he's put his reading glasses on. A sure sign he's in fix-it mode.

Gawd, how I hate needing to be fixed.

"How do we cure this?" Jace studies the images. "Are we now talking surgery?"

Dr. Madison scoots closer. "It depends. Are the two of you planning on having children?"

"Yes," I blurt out just as Jace drawls, "We haven't decided."

We look at each other, confused.

"Why don't I give you some information about what your choices are given what I'm seeing. We can schedule a follow-up appointment for next week after you've had time to discuss," she says without judgement. I guess she's used to delivering not-so-good news to couples who aren't necessarily on the same page.

We don't say anything as we wait for the elevator. Not on the ride down. When we reach our destination, I step into the garage and bolt toward the Range Rover. Before I can get into the passenger seat, Jace's palm smacks the window above my head to keep the door closed.

"Please, don't shut me out." His gravelly voice echoes in the cement enclosure.

I pull my coat around me tightly. "I'm not planning on it."

He clicks the fob and unlocks the door for me. I slip into the seat while he moves around the car to sit behind the wheel. Resting his elbows on the steering wheel, he buries his face in his hand.

"I'm the one with the fucked-up reproductive system, don't be so gloomy." I make a sad, pathetic attempt at a joke.

"Alex." He looks at me with tears in his eyes. "This isn't funny."

I sulk back into my seat and cross my arms. "Of course it isn't funny. There's a solution. I'm going to have the surgery and then I'll be fine."

"No. You heard what she said, we don't know if that's an option." Jace's mouth is set in a grim line. His lip quivers. Just slightly.

I can't help it. I can't hold back. Jace is sad. I'm devastated. I burst into tears.

He wraps his arm around my shoulders and cuddles me. "Hey, it's going to be okay. We'll get through this."

"If it's possible, I'm willing to take the risk, Jace."

"What about what I want?" He leans back and withdraws his arm. "I want to spend the rest of my life with you. I want us to get married. To raise Lena. To get certification for the ranch so we can do real therapy work. Go on tour for a couple months a year with the band to pay the bills. It would be an excellent, fulfilling life. One we'll build together."

I reach for his hand and thread my fingers through his. "Jace, stop. All I'm focused on is getting rid of this crap inside my body so we at least have the chance to get pregnant. Don't tell me you don't want a baby too."

"She said that if you take a combination of birth control pills and hormones the symptoms might resolve themselves." I'll give it to him, nothing much slips past him.

"And she said hormones might put me into menopause. I wouldn't be able to have a baby. So, it's a worse option than having surgery."

He shakes his head. "Poppy, she flat-out said there are lots of risks if you go under the knife."

"Look. We're not going to solve this today. Let's pick up Lena. I want to do the Christmas stuff." I buckle my seatbelt and stare straight ahead. I'm furious at Jace. Who does he think he is? It's my body. My decision.

"Poppy?"

I say nothing.

"Poppy."

I keep my eyes fixed on the window.

"Poppy."

"What do you want me to say?" I bellow. "Did you see those images? That's inside me. I feel disgusting. I feel utterly and totally damaged. Can you please give me a little time to process all of this? Let me absorb? You're coming at me and telling me what I can and cannot do. I know you're scared. I know you mean well. I'm begging you. Please stop before you say something you won't be able to unsay."

"But…"

I whip my head. "Jace. I don't want you to fix me. Right now, all I want is for you to just love me."

He gulps. "I do love you. More than anything."

"I love you too. So can we please get Lena and have a fun day? No matter what's going on with me, I'm her mother. She deserves to have the day we promised her and I'm going to give it to her. Okay?" I place my hand on his knee. "Let's get out of this parking lot. Please."

Jace nods and starts the engine. We head toward my mom's house to pick up our daughter.

I'm a fighter, that's what I know.

So is Jace.

We're both used to making things happen. For creating our own magic.

I want to expand my family with Jace.

And no alien invasion is going to get in my way.

Chapter Eight

A Week or so ater

WELL, WE'VE GONE ALL out on Christmas shit this year.

Alex insisted. She doubled down after our visit with the specialist. Oh, I know it's a diversion. For God's sake, our house looks like it's exploded with holiday decorations. Alex, Becca, and Jen have covered nearly every bush and shrub with twinkly lights. Inflatable Santa and his inflatable reindeer are tacked up to the roof of the barn.

Poor Mitch got his picture taken wearing an elf costume, much to the delight of Lena.

I suppose it's all worth it to see my daughter gleefully enjoy the holidays. It's a far cry from last year when I was agonizing over whether or not I was her biological father. Back then, I didn't want her to be mine.

Now, I can't imagine my life without her.

Since her appointment, Alex has been on a low dose of hormones which, together with her birth control pills, seem to be just barely controlling her pain. At least her cramps aren't nearly at the level they were.

I still feel conflicted. I didn't want her to go through invasive surgery. Not if it's only to give us a chance to conceive a baby I'm not sure she wants.

On the other hand, Dr. Madison has given her some hope and has been clear about the challenges. Surgery will allow her to get a sense of the depth and location of her endometriosis, which from the ultrasound seems to be everywhere. She also plans to remove the lesions using badass cutting-edge techniques.

Gah. What do I know? When Alex asked me how I'd feel if my balls were ravaged with welts, I took her point.

As I'm settling into the idea, I don't see any reason for her not to get it done, I guess.

All I want is for us to grow old together.

I can't lose her.

I won't risk losing her.

All of these thoughts swirl through my mind as I steer my truck toward home. A couple of hours ago, I went out for an errand and found myself thirty miles away. I needed to take a drive to clear my head. Not the smartest move when we have guests coming.

Mitch greets me at the end of our long, gravel driveway. I scratch him behind the ears and notice Zane waiting for me on the porch. No matter where he goes, he looks like a rock star. Today is no exception. He lowers his aviator glasses when he jumps up to greet me. "My man. What took you so long? You missed lunch. Fee left your food in the fridge."

"Sorry I'm so late. I had to go to a store three towns over to find bubble-gum ice cream." I grab the grocery bag from the passenger seat. "Who the hell even likes this shit?"

Zane snatches the bag from my hand and peeks inside. "Uh, everyone."

"Where are all of the ladies?" I glance around the yard.

"In the barn. They're getting the horses ready for pictures." Zane follows me into the house, where I put the ice cream in the freezer and some cupcakes on the counter.

I hand him a cold beer. "Whatcha doin' for Christmas?"

"Fee's cooking. Faye will be there." He rolls his eyes. "Carter and Mom too."

"They're back together then?"

He shrugs. "Who the hell knows. She's not making it easy on him. My dad's like a lost puppy around her." Zane begins to fidget. He's not a man who can stay still exceedingly long.

"Well, let's see what's up. Who knows what will happen if we leave them alone this long," I joke, holding the door ajar for him.

We creep as silently as possible into the barn, mainly so we can spy a little. The sight is breathtaking if I do say so myself. Alex, Fiona, Mia, and Lena are in the modest indoor arena we just finished. Alex is working with Samantha, a gorgeous little palomino who'd been neglected and left for dead at a ranch a couple of towns over. Gloria, our first rescue, stands close by.

"What is she doing?" Zane whispers.

I watch Alex in awe. Ever since I took her to Cavalia, she's spent hours training the horses. "It's called liberty training. She doesn't use any tack, halters, or ropes. She's working to give the horse a sense of choice rather than the old-school method of 'breaking' them in. The technique gives both Alex and the horse a sense of freedom. It helps her create a type of bond where she's able to train advanced horsemanship skills."

"You've taken to life out here, J-man." Zane doesn't take his eyes off Alex's impressive show.

"I have."

"Daddy!" Mia spots Zane and comes barreling toward us. He scoops her up in his arms and blows a giant zerbit on her cheek.

I wave over to the ladies. "Hey, got the stuff. It's in the house."

"Took you long enough. It's time to dress up the horses for the pictures." Alex picks up Lena and walks over to us. Samantha follows and stands at her side.

Fee saunters up to us wearing a black cowboy hat over two bright-pink pigtails. "I can't get over how cool you are, Alex. This liberty horse stuff is fucking awesome."

"Well, I can't even boil an egg, so we're equally badass, just in different ways." Alex rubs her nose against Lena's. "Right, Lena? Girls are badasses."

I take Lena from her, laughing. "So, we're just embracing the curse words now?"

"I started swearing at a very young age, and I turned out pretty good." Fee winks at me before planting a big kiss on Zane's lips.

He hooks his thumb into the beltloop of her jeans and tugs her toward him. "One more of those, wife."

As they kiss again, Alex glances at me and looks away. Fuck. I'm so goddamn horny. Ever since that fateful doctor appointment, we haven't had sex. Nearly three whole weeks. Nothing. Nada. She hasn't even wanted me to give her the cure.

It's not for a lack of me trying, either. I mean, I want Alex literally all the time. Ever since we saw what was growing inside her, she's pulled away a bit. She said she's just not feeling sexy.

Which sucks.

At least today, she's back to herself. She's always at her most grounded when she's working with the horses.

Well, that and spending time with the girls. In any event, it's the happiest she's been since we got the diagnosis.

"Okay, ladies. Should we go get the ribbon?" Alex dances and sashays toward Samantha. "Mia and Lena, let me show you."

Fiona, Zane, and I sit on stacks of hay and watch her patiently teach the girls how to brush the horses' manes and tails. Carefully, she demonstrates how to wrap red, green, and gold ribbon around sections of the mane and secure it in place with a colorful rubber band. She repeats the process with their tails. The girls giggle when they copy what she's doing. One thing's for sure, they're mesmerized by Alex and her way with animals.

"Da Da!" Lena jumps up and down and points to Samantha's completed mane. "Smantha hath cwithmith wibbon!"

"It's beautiful, sweetheart." I circle around to inspect the decorated horses.

Zane shadows me with Fee close behind. "Dude, this is awesome." He runs his fingers along Gloria's mane.

Fiona flings her arm around Alex. "You are such a natural mother, Alex. You're so wonderful with the girls."

"Ah, thanks, Fee," Alex says quietly. She coughs and looks away, but I see a bit of sheen in her eyes. I run my hand along her back and kiss her head. "I'll take them outside if you want to get them ready for our holiday pictures."

While Alex and Fiona take the girls inside to change, I lead the horses out to the pasture and snap some sample shots facing the house and then the woods to ascertain where the best location is. Zane, my interim model, cheeses for the camera and flashes rock horns with his ringed fingers.

"You're going to have more kids, aren't you?" Zane pats Gloria's cheek. "It's like you two were born for this."

I don't answer for a minute, probably a minute too long. "Uh…"

"I get it. I can't wait, though. I want Fee and me to have a baby. She keeps putting me off, though. She won't go off birth control. Says the restaurant is her baby for now. It sucks because now that Ty and Zoey are trying, I thought it would be excellent timing for us too. Think about it. We could all have kids who grow up together. I loved Connor's idea of bringing the families with us when we tour. LTZ could have our own traveling elementary school," Zane rambles.

"Uh, yeah. That'd be cool." I'm not going to divulge anything about our situation to Zane. Not that I don't trust him, but I don't know how much she's told Fee.

Zane toes the ground. "Tell me the truth, you're not going to quit the band are you?"

"What?" My head whips around to see if he's serious. He is.

"You're just so blasé when you used to be so into it." He meets my gaze. "I get why Connor is hesitant. His dad isn't doing well. He has twin babies. Same with Ty, he's newly married and trying for a kid. I even get why me and Fiona need time because the restaurant is a bit all-consuming and Mia's in school now. But you? Becca and Jen can watch the ranch. Lena's not quite two. You guys could easily mobilize and globetrot as a family."

His assumptions about our lives annoy me, even though he's partially correct. "You've got it all figured out, huh?"

"C'mon." He furrows his brow and crosses his muscled arms over his chest.

I'm saved from answering by Mia and Lena running toward us in green-and-gold Christmas dresses, white tights and black patent-leather shoes. "Don't you ladies look beautiful." I scoop up my daughter and Zane picks up his.

Alex and Fiona wear matching black-velvet V-neck shirts and jeans. I help position the girls on each horse and Alex and Fee beside them. I snap a bunch of pictures with distinctive setups so we have a lot to choose from.

"These are gorgeous." Fiona grabs my phone when we're done and scrolls through, stopping to airdrop a bunch of shots to herself. "Will you post them?"

"Where? I'm not doing the band social anymore." I pull Lena down from Samantha and cuddle her to my chest. She's exhausted and nestles into my neck and starts sucking her thumb.

Zane helps Mia off Gloria. "Dude, she's talking to Alex."

Alex shakes her head at me and takes my phone from Fiona. "Yeah, I'll post on the ranch IG. I'd love to make a tradition with all the kids, don't you think?"

"Absolutely. It will be so awesome to watch them grow up and have this experience every year." Fee flips through her phone, checking out the shots. "What a fun day, you guys. I needed this break badly."

Fiona and Zane bring the girls in for their bubble-gum ice cream and cupcakes while Alex and I sort out the horses. We visit for a bit and after they leave, I eat the lunch leftovers and we watch Disney+ until Lena conks out. I put her to bed and rejoin Alex on the couch. She's fired up the latest season of Heartland on Netflix. I cuddle her to me.

"You deserve to be a mother, if that's what you want, Poppy," I whisper against her hair. "I'm sorry if I haven't seemed supportive. I just can't stand the thought of anything happening to you."

She tightens her arms around me. "I never thought I'd want it. You know that. I didn't mean to change my mind but it's how I feel. Dr. Madison seems to think she can make it happen."

"Yeah, but you're not talking about it to me. I'm trying not to annoy you, but all this stuff is a lot to take in. I hope you know I'm here for you. I wish you would tell me how you're feeling instead of bottling it up." I wind my finger around a lock of her hair.

She tilts her face to mine. Her full lips glisten. I bend my neck to kiss her. Little nibbles. Slips of the tongue. My dick fills immediately. My hands roam across her back. Her taut waist. She sits up and faces me. "I know. I'm sorry. I miss you."

"I miss you too."

"All of this is messing with me. I feel disgusting. I've seen pictures of endometriosis...it's inside me."

"Don't you dare say you're disgusting. Not when you are the most beautiful woman on the planet," I interrupt. I can't listen to her feel insecure about something she can't control.

She buries her face in her hands.

I know what she needs.

And I'm going to be the one to give it to her.

Always.

Chapter Nine

The Same Day

JACE'S FINGERS LACE THROUGH mine and he pulls my hands from my face.

"You're ravishing." He kisses my forehead.

"You're pure joy." He kisses each of my temples.

"You're light and love." His lips touch mine.

"You're my everything," he murmurs against my lips as he brings our clasped hands together behind his back. My nipples harden when my chest presses into his muscled pecs. I've missed this. Us. I've been in a fog ever since I found out what I was dealing with.

I'm not me anymore. I'm a shell. An insecure woman whose ever-present thought is how badly I'm damaged. How gross I feel. Negative self-talk flows through my brain in a nonstop loop. Whispers of why a man like Jace—who is not only a perfect physical specimen, but the most capable, intelligent, funny man I've ever known, not to mention rich and famous—would want to stay with me. A not-quite-thirty-year-old woman on the precipice of what could be infertility.

His sweet words help, but don't drown out these voices.

"Why?" I'm breathless between his kisses.

"Why what, Poppy?" He releases my hands and brings his palms to the sides of my face. Tenderly, he strokes my cheeks with his thumbs. His crazily green eyes bore into mine. Questioning my question. Seeking...something. Something I'm not sure how to give him.

"Why..." The words get stuck in my throat. I'm such an emotional basket case these days. It sucks to not feel like yourself. Weak is not something I've ever been.

This feeling is so unfamiliar. I've held it together—by a string—all day, and the effort's taken it out of me.

He draws me to him by wrapping strong arms around my back. "I don't know how to help you. How to make you see that no matter what, you're perfect. That I want to be with you forever."

"But I'm all over the map. I'm not the person you fell in love with. I'm not fun anymore. I'm broody. My body is betraying me. The one thing most women take for granted—I took for granted—is now a huge unknown. You can be with anyone, Jace. Why do you want me..."

Jace pulls back abruptly, his eyebrows knit, and he crosses his arms protectively across his chest. "Jesus, stop saying that. When I was fucked up over the paternity stuff, I was an absolute asshole to be around. You stuck by my side even when I pushed you away. Why on earth would you think I wouldn't stick by you when you're going through a hard time?"

"So you feel obligated." I can't help uttering these hurtful words. Immediately, I regret what I've said. Well, regret is probably too strong. I do want to know if there's some small part of him that does feel that way.

He shakes his head and looks at the porch. "God, Poppy. I'm pouring my heart out to you. Telling you my deepest thoughts about how you make me feel, and you think that equates to being obligated?"

"Do you, though?" I squeeze my eyes shut so I can't see his face.

"No, I don't feel fucking obligated. But I do fucking miss you." He scrubs the stubble on his chin with his hand. "I don't mean to sound like an asshole, but is it possible for you to stop with the woebegone stuff? You're still you. If you could see what I saw...the way you were with the girls today? That was one hundred percent Alex fucking LeRoux. Plus, we don't know anything definite yet. Maybe stop imagining the worst-case scenario?"

I want to shrink into myself because I hate how insecure I'm being. I hate how much this diagnosis is affecting my mental health. I don't answer him because I can't find the words.

Jace blows out a long breath and leans back, slipping his arm back around me. "If you're having issues with depression, then let's set up some time with Lisa Kinkaid. Or someone else you feel comfortable with. It's totally understandable, Poppy. I'm sorry I'm pushing you if you're not ready."

I grip his wrist. "No. I'm sad, but I don't think I'm depressed. I'm mostly scared. Or maybe even angry at myself for not dealing with this sooner. For possibly creating a situation that can't be reversed."

We both lean back on the couch. It's such a relief to talk this out and not keep it inside. "What I was trying to tell you very ineloquently is that I'll honor your wishes." Jace's voice is calmer now, soothing. "I believe it when you say you've changed your mind about having kids. I want to stop being scared shitless so I can support you having the surgery. There's nothing I want other than to put all of this behind us. Mostly, I just want you to know that, as far as I'm concerned, this diagnosis doesn't define you. It doesn't define us."

"I just want it out of my bawd-eeeee," I groan, drawing the word out. "I want it G.O.N.E gone."

"Okay. I'm on board. Let's get it gone." He traces my eyebrow with his finger.

On a whim, I scramble to straddle him. Without missing a beat, he grips my ass and pulls me flush against him.

I wrap my arms around his neck and bury my face in his hair. "I love you, Jace Deveraux."

"Thank God. I was beginning to wonder." He smirks as he trails a hand down my back and deftly pulls up my shirt. I raise my arms above my head and he yanks it all the way off, leaving me topless. My nipples pucker into tight nuggets from the cool air. Or, maybe in anticipation of us finding our way back to who we once were.

Our mouths slam together with sloppy, hurried kisses. A mash of soft lips and sharp teeth. He nips my chin and I push his face to my breast. I want everything he has to give me. Jace's lips kiss down my throat, then latch on to my nipple. He sucks hard then swirls his tongue around it soothingly. A nibble. A lick. A suck. Each so incredibly tantalizing as he makes his way across my chest and worships my other breast with equal enthusiasm.

Oh, how I needed this. Another moment in time like we used to have. Before things got so complicated.

I grip his waist, slide my hands up under his armpits and clutch his back to give me enough leverage to grind my core against his erection. My knees squeeze his hips. My head lolls back as I get lost in the dual stimulation. He cups each breast, thumbing my nipples to keep them taut. He kisses his way back up to my face and devours my lips again. Gawd, the unbridled pleasure that washes over my body.

Pleasure I've denied myself for too long.

When he stops abruptly, my eyes spring open to find him studying me. "Alex, I need you. Need this. But are you on board? I want to fuck you hard. Really hard."

"God, yes." I cant my hips to create friction with his cock. I want to show him how okay I am with all of this. He presses on my lower back so there's no space between our lower bodies. He's harder than a titanium rod. A porch light flicks on over at Becca and Jen's. "Maybe we should take this inside."

I'm barely able to grab my shirt to cover myself before Jace drags me through the door, past the kitchen, the cats, and into our bedroom. He locks it behind us, we kick off our shoes and in one precise move he sheds his hoodie and undershirt to stalk me like a cheetah. Giggling, I back up and toss the shirt at him. "Oh, is that how it is?" He pounces and we flop to the bed.

Bare chest to bare chest, the heat between us is like a roaring campfire. Our hands roam and grope. He reaches between us to unbuckle my belt. I fumble with his in the race to de-clothe ourselves. He manages to get my jeans unbuttoned and wastes no time slipping his fingers under my panties and inside me. I'm sopping wet, he has no trouble finding the magic spot inside, just past my G-spot. Jace sucks and licks my earlobe in cadence with his rubs, flicks, and presses.

Oh, I know what he's up to, Jace loves doing this sure-thing rockstar trick on me. Occasionally, when he goes all in on this technique, I squirt. When I do, it's like he's won the lottery. Soaking him is like a special prize to my sexy drummer.

My orgasm crashes through me so hard my teeth chatter. He withdraws his fingers for a moment to tug my jeans and panties off. I use the opportunity to sit up and slide his track pants down his hips. His cock bobs against his cut abs a mere millimeter from my lips. Without a second thought, I suck him down my throat. Swallow around his crown and work my way up his shaft. He grips my cheeks and fucks my face a bit, it's so intense. So incredibly intense.

"If I don't stop now, I'm going to come." He pulls out and presses my chest to the bed so I'm lying back against the pillows. I allow my knees to fall against the sheets, giving him an unobstructed view of my pussy. When I'm this wet, he loves the view. I pinch my nipples and lick my lips. "You're so goddamn perfect, Alex." Jace reinserts his fingers to the hilt. I dig my heels into the bed and wait for magic.

Spreading me with the fingers of his other hand, he bends to wiggle his tongue on my clit while manipulating my secret spot. Ah, holy hell. Electricity shoots through my entire body. An invisible wire of such monumental pleasure it should be illegal. Gawd, it probably is illegal. My second orgasm is followed by a third, fourth, and fifth in succession, each consuming me with pleasure that cannot be described. He is relentless, rubbing the spot. I bear down. My head thrashes. My hands clench his shoulders when I gush all over his face, his fingers, and the bed. I shove my fist against my mouth to try to stifle the sound of the keening moan I'm emitting from deep in my soul.

Every nerve is alive. Every sense is heightened. Jace sits back on his knees and smiles, his face coated with...well, me. He leans over and shoves his hands under my ass, pulling me on top of him so I'm basically in his lap. He guides his cock inside me just as I wrap my arms around his neck and bury my face in his hair. He's smells so amazing. Sandalwood and sea. Jace controls the pace, slamming me down on him. Faster. Harder. I hang on for the ride. "Fuck me, Jace. God, harder. Harder."

We haven't fucked like this for so long. Even on the night of our engagement.

It's cleansing.

Jace changes tactics and slows things way down so we're moving as one. Our bodies are smashed together tightly. My legs are locked around his butt. His wide palms span my back and press me into him. His cock is so deep inside me. We stare into each other's eyes. I've not felt this connected to him since my diagnosis, but it's not his fault. He's my everything. "I love you, Jace. I hope you know how much you make my life complete."

"Poppy, there's no limit to how much I love you." Jace tightens his arms around me and grips both of my ass cheeks to pick up the pace again. He rolls us over and fucks me with abandon. I watch his thick cock pound into me, which makes me even wetter than I am already. The entire room smells like our sex. I watch his orgasm tear through his body, it's so fucking hot I can't even stand it. First his jaw goes slack, then his tattooed arms lock on either side of me. His eyes squeeze shut as he throws his head back and I'm filled with his come, the supply of which never seems to end.

I can't help but clench around him as I come for the sixth time, an absolute record. We stay joined for a while, not for any reason. Well, unless you factor in neither of us can move.

"We're pros at that." Ten minutes later, I'm finally able to speak again. He's collapsed on top of me, so I stroke his hair.

I can feel him smile against my chest. "Fuck yeah, we are."

"I know you're scared about all of this, but I trust Dr. Madison. I'm going to be okay. I'm too young and healthy to just give up, you know?" I say softly.

He rolls off me and cuddles me to his chest. "You really want a baby?"

"I'd like to have the option. Or at least the chance, maybe."

"Okay." His gravelly voice is filled with conviction. "I'm on board."

"Really?"

He gazes down at me. "I'd never hold you back from something you wanted. Never."

I lean up for a kiss. This man is perfect. In each and every way.

I hope my body will be fixed up soon. It's imperative. He deserves everything. Because the last thing I'll ever do? Drag Jace down.

I'll die before I'd let that happen.

Chapter Ten

Six Weeks Later

IT'S LITERALLY FREEZING OUTSIDE. When we woke up this morning, it was still pitch black. About an inch of snow covered the entire property. Alex's mom is staying in our guest room so she can stay with Lena until we get home.

I'm bundled up with multiple layers, a weatherproof jacket, gloves, and a thick wool skull cap. Alex is basically dressed as my twin. God knows why we're standing outside on the upper deck of the ferry with freezing rain pelting us in the face as the traces of eerie, gray late-winter light become visible.

I'm not asking questions, though. I followed Alex out here. If she wants to be outside today, I'm going to be next to her.

The air's so cold, my eyelashes are starting to freeze. I bury my face in her neck and pull her tighter against my chest. She turns in my arms and slams her lips against mine. Shoves her tongue in my mouth. I return her kiss tenfold.

We're both scared shitless.

The past couple of days haven't been the most fun. In preparation for her laparoscopy to explore and remove her endometriosis lesions, Alex choked down a gallon of foul liquid to clean out her system. None of it has been the most pleasant experience for any of us in the house. This morning, she scrubbed her entire body in the shower using special anti-bacterial soap. She hasn't been able to eat for two days either, and a hangry Alex is no joke.

As Dr. Madison explained the procedure, she'll make incisions in Alex's belly and insert a camera to get a better look at the lesions. Apparently, it's fairly non-invasive surgery and it will serve a double purpose because she'll remove as much as she can. The samples will get analyzed. Hopefully, if all goes well, we'll know the extent of what Alex is dealing with.

If all goes really well, her symptoms might be drastically reduced, and we can resume our life normally. Maybe even have a baby.

"It's going to be fine. I know it." Alex's entire body is shivering. Her teeth chatter.

"Of course it will. Now, Poppy? We're going inside. Nothing is smart about catching pneumonia before surgery." I steer her toward the glass door to the cafeteria where I buy myself a large cup of coffee.

Aside from the early-bird commuters, we're alone on this ferry so we grab a booth and stare out at the gray sky and choppy waves while I sip my coffee. Alex, of course, can't eat or drink anything before surgery, but she insisted I needed to caffeinate.

She's so right.

"She wants to remove the cyst on my ovary. I might lose it." Alex's cheeks are bright pink, but at least she seems to be warming up.

"I know. You still have one perfectly healthy ovary." I've read so much about the condition; I like to be prepared.

Alex looks down at her black Frye boots. "When I'm recovered, I think we should try for a baby right away. I'm almost thirty. My eggs are going to start drying up. I don't want to wait and miss what might be a very narrow window."

"Yes, you're ancient. We definitely need to start the second you recover. Does that mean we get to have sex all the time?" I peer over the lip of my cup at her.

She sticks her tongue out at me. "I'm just being realistic."

"Why don't we take this in steps. Until we're through today, all I can wrap my head around is keeping you safe. And healthy."

"I just want to ask when we can start trying." Alex gazes back out the window. "In case it makes a difference."

I reach over and grab her mittened hand in my gloved one. "Yes. Let's ask everything so there's no questions left unasked. It's a terrific idea."

She looks at me, her eyes glisten just a bit because she's working hard to hold her emotions at bay. "Okay then."

The drive to the clinic is not even ten minutes from the ferry. We're ushered in. I wait as Alex is cleaned and swabbed and prepped and I'm allowed in for a brief consult with her doctor before the procedure begins.

"Alex, before we get started I just want to remind you there is currently no cure for endometriosis." Dr. Madison stands at the foot of Alex's hospital bed. I sit next to her, holding her hand. "The goal of this laparoscopic surgery is to improve your symptoms, do everything we can to preserve your fertility."

Alex is drowning in her hospital gown. She looks tiny. Scared. I'm scared too, but I'm not going to show it. I'm here to be my Poppy's rock. "We've read all the materials you've provided. We want to do this. At the very least, Alex can't live with the kind of pain she's experiencing."

"I agree wholeheartedly." Dr. Madison is kind but efficient. Clearly, she's done hundreds of these surgeries. "You've signed the consent forms, but I just want to confirm I have your permission to excise the damaged tissue and the cyst. There's a risk that you'll lose that ovary but as we discussed, it doesn't appear your other ovary is affected."

"I understand." Alex nods. "It is what it is, if it's got to come out, we'll deal with it."

I'm allowed to give her a kiss before I'm ushered out into a waiting room with a couple other guys. One of them does a double take, so I pull down my skull cap and take the seat at the farthest end of the room.

Minutes later, he's beside me. "Dude, LTZ is my favorite band. Can I get a selfie to post to IG?"

Jesus. I don't mind having fans, especially because of all the guys I get bothered the least, but in the motherfucking clinic? "Sure, but I'd appreciate it if you didn't tag me. Obviously, we're both in a medical facility..."

"No problem." He tilts his camera toward us. I don't smile, but I don't shoot a laser dart at him with my eyes either. "I can't fuckin' believe I met Jace Deveraux. What are you here for?"

I can't help but paste on a smile. "It's nice to meet you too. If you don't mind, I've got to go make a call."

I stand and stalk toward the nurses' station. It takes a hot minute for the young woman with long, black hair to glance up. Her face reddens and her eyes widen. "Oh. Mr. Deveraux. How can I help you?"

"Is there anywhere else I can wait for my fiancée?" I flash her my rock-star smile. "I don't want to be a pain, but…"

"Oh, yes. Of course." She flushes an even brighter red. I'm used to this when I'm on the road. It's just been a while and it feels just as weird as it did when LTZ started getting famous.

She leads me to a tiny, but private, waiting area and assures me that she'll let Dr. Madison's team know where to find me. There's a green vinyl couch that's calling my name, but before I relax, I call home and check in with my sister and Alex's mom. Once I'm assured all is well, I lie down and immediately fall asleep.

"Mr. Deveraux?" Someone is shaking me awake. I whirl around, unable to get my bearings until I realize where I am. My discombobulation is replaced with a bolt of adrenaline and I'm up like a shot.

"How is she?" I scrub my eyes with my fists and see the dark-haired woman hovering above me "Can I see her?"

She takes a step back. "She's in recovery. Dr. Madison will be here in ten-to-fifteen minutes."

Exactly fifteen minutes later, the doctor knocks and enters the room. Her face is unreadable. "Jace, I have some good news and a little bit of bad news."

My heart feels like it has been pushed off a cliff. I try to hide it. "Oh? Maybe start with the bad?"

"We weren't able to save her ovary, and the fallopian tube was completely infiltrated with lesions. We were weren't able to save it either."

My breath heaves. We knew this was possible. Still doesn't make hearing about it very easy. "Okay. What's the good news?"

She smiles. "We got almost all of it. And her remaining ovary and fallopian tube look healthy. Her uterus too. After recovery, I have every hope she'll be pain-free and ready to try for a baby."

My eyes squeeze shut. I know Alex is going to be sad about losing part of her reproductive organs, but we mentally prepared for this. Overall, this is a great outcome.

Dr. Madison places her hand on my shoulder. "I'll come get you when she starts to come to. I think it's best if she stays here tonight, so maybe make whatever arrangements you need while you wait."

We were prepared for this possibility too. I call Alex's mom again to give her the news. Call Jen. Then my folks. I pace a bit. Play a game on my phone. Finally, when I get bored just sitting here, I break down and turn on the television on the wall. I'm not paying attention to the 24-hour news channel, but the voices are a welcome distraction.

Close to two hours later, a nurse fetches me and leads me to Alex's room. Her eyes blink open when I approach her bed. "Hey."

"You still woozy?" I sit next to her and stroke the hand that isn't hooked up to a bag of fluid.

"Mmm." Her eyes flutter closed. "Sleepy."

"You can sleep, Poppy. I'll be right here." I squeeze her hand.

"Where's Lena?" She smacks her lips.

I bring the cup of water with a paper straw to her lips and she sucks down some water. "She's with your mom. She's fine. You and I are going to stay here tonight."

She nods and dozes off. I brush her blonde hair from her face. She's angelic. I'm so relieved she's going to be okay. I resolve to do everything in my power to help her recover. Then I'm marrying her. And if she still wants a baby? Well, we're going to have a hell of a time making one.

Alex wakes up again a couple hours later when Dr. Madison comes back to check on her. She's fairly alert and clearly starting to feel the effects of the procedure. A nurse hands her a miniature cup with a pill in it and a glass of water.

"We were in surgery for about five hours, Alex." The doctor taps her clipboard annoyingly as she explains the procedure in greater detail. "I'm prescribing pain medication to get you through the next few days. Then you can switch back to Tylenol or Advil until you're healed. What's most important is to rest and avoid excess strain on your abdomen. That means no lifting, pushing, or pulling heavy objects, or riding horses for at least six weeks."

"I'll make sure of it." I wring my hands and then shake them out. Knowing Alex, she'll try to be back up and running by the weekend.

Alex's eyes begin to drift shut again. Someone wheels a cot into the room for me to sleep on. It's not even seven p.m. and I'm exhausted. And starving. Who knew what an emotional strain it would be to sit around all day while the love of your life went through surgery.

"Go get something to eat and call Lena before her bedtime." Alex's voice is faint but decisive. "I don't want her to see me in the hospital."

"I will. Then I'll come back here and sleep by your side tonight." I pet her head. She nods and makes a shooing motion toward the door.

As hard as it is for me to leave, even for a little bit, I realize that Alex needs a little time on her own. She's clearly equally parts grateful and annoyed at my hovering.

So I do as she requests.

I read my daughter a bedtime story on FaceTime. Then devour a spicy noodle dish at a Thai restaurant across the street from the clinic. An hour later, I crawl into the cot, and watch her peacefully sleep.

As I drift off, I feel so incredibly lucky.

And grateful.

It's been an incredibly scary day.

Now, everything's going to be okay.

Chapter Eleven

A Few Days Later

I SHOULD FEEL GRATEFUL.

And I do...

It's just I'm also incredibly sad. I hate feeling this way, but my emotions are all over the place. Dr. Madison told me that it was normal to mourn the loss of body parts. Important parts I took for granted my entire life.

God, how cavalier I was when I was younger. To me, the idea I had full control over my ability to reproduce was a foregone conclusion.

I cringe thinking about some of my first conversations with Jace. Like when I casually tossed out the idea of getting my tubes tied so I could have sex without getting pregnant. The way I reacted when I thought I was knocked up after that sex-crazed summer in Europe.

Gawd, I cried with relief when the test was negative. Then broke up with him in the next breath.

No wonder Jace was so hurt. No wonder he's been so skeptical of my desire to get pregnant now.

I'm not a woo-woo girl. I know my words and actions didn't cause the endometriosis. Or the fact I lost an ovary and fallopian tube. Why then is there an aggravating little voice inside my head that taunts me?

You manifested this.

I push the thought away and sigh. It's no secret I'm struggling both mentally and physically from what turned out to be major surgery. My jaw clenches just thinking about how long I'm going to be out of commission. It sucks. I can't even sit up due to the stabbing pain in my abdomen. Even still, I'm determined to get through as fast as possible. Like religiously following my post-op instructions. Making Jace help me walk to the bathroom and back because Dr. Madison told me moving would help me heal faster.

"Are you up?" My mom peeks into my room. "I've made breakfast."

My appetite hasn't quite returned yet, but the greasy smell of bacon and eggs is appealing. "I'll try and eat. Thanks momikins." She sets a tray on the nightstand and feeds me delicious bites until I'm full.

Mom kisses my temple. "How's the pain?"

"I'm insanely bloated. My incisions are sore. It hurts to pee. Oh, and it feels like Freddy Krueger sliced my uterus into shreds." I give her a big, cheesy smile and pair it with a thumbs up.

"So, better then?" Jace enters the bedroom with a brown paper bag.

Mom grabs the breakfast tray and passes him on the way to the kitchen. "Her color's returning and her sass is back. I'd say she's better."

"Your antibiotics, madam." Jace sits at the foot of the bed and pulls out a package of tablets. "Ten days of these puppies and you'll be in the clear."

I swallow the pill and reposition myself to pet Benjamin and Franklin, who've taken up residence on Jace's side of the bed since I returned home, and he's been relegated to a guest room for the time being. "Aren't you two the best medicine? Balls of purring fur who don't make fun of the infertile girl."

"Well, that is not funny." Jace stands up and looks out the window, which overlooks the pasture.

"Jace, I'm sorry. You're right."

He turns and resumes sitting at the edge of the bed. Places his hand on my hip. I reach down and cover his hand with mine. He sighs heavily. "Look, I'm the one who's sorry. I don't want to tell you what you can and cannot say. There's no right or wrong here. This happened to you. It's just...you're not infertile. It hurts me when you joke about it."

"It must be hard to watch me go through all this." I thread my fingers with his.

His eyes fill with tears. "You have no idea."

"I hate to do this to you, but I have to pee and change my pads. The bleeding is insane." I wince. As embarrassing as it is, I can't do my business without Jace yet. Not that he's made me feel weird about it. He's been incredibly cool.

I almost feel—safe?

"Stop apologizing, Poppy. For now, my job is to get you healed. Well, and obviously take care of Lena." He jumps up and springs into action.

Half hour later, we've navigated my messy business, he's given me a sponge bath, washed my hair and dressed me. Fresh underwear...there's nothing like it.

I'm clean. I'm cozy. I'm back in bed, with a Yeti of warm peppermint tea in hand because it's helpful to reduce my swelling. "Happy Valentine's Day, right?" I purse my lips at him like I'm posing for an old-school IG photo.

"You know what? It is the best Valentine's Day I've ever had. You're on the mend. Your cramps are going to be gone. I get to spend the rest of my life with you." Jace takes my tea from me and taps the container three times in succession. "Glass. Half. Full."

"Gawd, I'm turning into Debbie Downer, aren't I?" I scrunch up my nose at the thought.

"Eh? I was mentally prepared for it. Dr. Madison told me that as part of the surgery, you'd have a complete personality transplant. I'm still on board. For now." He smirks.

"For me, aside from being a weepy, snarky mess, the worst thing right now is the gas pains." During the procedure, Dr. Madison pumped my stomach full of gas to be able to see the endometriosis and cysts better. "It's trapped in places I didn't expect. My knee and ankle are killing me."

Jace rubs the places that are aching very softly. "Drink the tea. It will help."

"You're incredible, you know. Wanna get married?" I smile, hoping it doesn't look like a grimace.

"I do." He grins, almost shyly.

My eyes are a bit heavy because the meds are kicking in. "I mean it."

"I'm counting on it," I hear him say before I doze off.

Sometime later, I become aware of Jace sound asleep on the double-sized chair next to me. He must have moved it into the bedroom next to my side of the bed while I was asleep. Lena is curled up in his lap, sucking her thumb. She's awake but quiet. Her aquamarine eyes watch me curiously.

I wave to her with my pinkie.

A dazzling smile takes over her face. She waves back to me. I motion her over. She slips from Jace's lap and tentatively shuffles over to me. when she's close enough for me to reach, I stroke her soft hair. "Hi, baby."

"Mama sick?"

"I'm almost better." I half roll over and pat the space next to me. "If you snuggle me, I'll get better faster."

Lena carefully climbs into bed next to me and I wrap my arm around her. She burrows her face into my neck. She smells like cookies and sunshine. Talk about the best medicine.

"Be careful with your mama. Remember I told you she has a boo boo in her belly." Jace gazes sleepily at us.

"Boo boo in Mama's bewwy." Lena grabs a lock of my hair and twists it with one little hand. Shoves her thumb in her mouth. Her eyes close and she drifts off not long after.

"I love you," Jace mouths.

I mouth it back.

He stealthily gets up and moves around to the far side of the bed. Plops the cats on the ground, climbs in behind us and spoons me. Swoops the duvet cover up to swaddle us in a warm, soft bubble.

I can't remember ever feeling more secure than in this bed-cocoon with my drummer and our little girl. Sure, I've lost a part of myself. But Jace's optimism is contagious. We have so much to look forward to in our future. I decide to forgive my younger self.

She was innocent. Naïve. Overconfident, perhaps.

I may not be that much older, but I've learned what's truly important.

It's all here with me now. In this bed.

And I'm never taking it for granted again.

Chapter Twelve

One Month Later

ALL I'VE DONE IS reflect since Poppy's surgery.

My conclusion? Endometriosis crept up on Alex slowly until it had her in a chokehold.

Illness, especially an invisible illness like hers, chips away at your psyche. That's for sure.

Ever since she recovered from her operation, Alex is like a new woman. Scratch that, she's reverted into her old playful carefree self. Words cannot describe how fucking amazing it is to see her light fully shine again.

She's so goddamn beautiful. Inside and out. I'm watching her teach Lena how to play fetch with Mitch through the kitchen window.

Moments like these are little slices of heaven to me.

The morning mist turns into a bit of a downpour, I mean it's the Pacific Northwest. There's a reason everything's so green here. I step out to the porch and shout, "You're gonna get wet."

Alex looks up at me, her smile wide as she points to her feet. "That's why they make these things called rain boots. Put yours on and join us. We have important business."

Of course, I can't resist. I put a thick hoodie on over my T-shirt, pull on my own pair of galoshes and bound down the stairs to my girls. "Okay, let's get to it, ladies."

"Da Da we splash the puddles." Lena reaches for my hand, which I take.

I look up at Alex and arch an eyebrow in question. She just laughs. "Is there anything better than puddle jumping?"

"I have no idea; I've never done it. I grew up with sisters, remember?" I crouch down to eye level with Lena. "Will you show your daddy how to do it?"

We trek across our entire property finding puddles to play in. Alex is the ringleader. We leap over clusters of puddles like an obstacle course. Use sticks to see how deep the big pools of water are. Toss rocks to see which ones make the biggest splash. Make little boats out of leaves and twigs to see if they'll float.

In the process, Alex teaches Lena about the trees and bushes that are indigenous to our environment. She shows Lena berries that are edible and warns her about the ones that are poisonous. We talk about the birds and bugs we come across. In the heavily wooded area that leads to a steep incline, we see a couple of deer.

Lena is utterly enthralled with the whole experience, but at this point we're all damp, even with the rain gear on. As we turn back to go back home, Alex runs up ahead and turns back to us. "Okay, now are you ready for the very best part of the whole day?"

Lena and I both yell out an enthusiastic, "Yes!"

"Follow my lead, and then we can take turns." She takes a running leap and jumps fully into a big puddle, causing it to splash mud all over her. "Wheeeeee!"

Before I can protest, Lena joyfully follows her and jumps into a smaller puddle. "Wheeeee!"

"C'mon, fancy pants." Alex motions to me. "Let's pop your puddle cherry."

Lena screams, "Poppa puddle! Poppa puddle!"

At least the puddle cherry meaning is lost on our two-year-old, I think as I jog toward them and launch myself with both feet into a huge puddle with my own "wheeeee!" I misjudge the depth, and the water and mud fly everywhere and fill my boots. I'm doused and soaked, and I don't care one bit. I maneuver out from the pool of water and pull off my boots to empty them before shoving them back on my wet feet.

"See? Isn't this the most fun ever?" Alex spins around and spreads her arms up wide to the sky. She sticks her tongue out to catch rain drops.

Lena copies her. "I taste the wain!"

"Does it taste good?" I mimic the two of them and stick my tongue out too.

Lena licks her lips. "Dewishus."

Alex and I catch each other's eye. The look that passes between us is magical. In an instant, everything we're feeling is expressed with a glance.

This is what life is about.

The three of us jump through puddles all the way home. Mitch, who has been with us for the entire journey but refrained from putting his precious paws in muddy water, is dirty, but still a thousand times cleaner than any of us. We're forced to strip on the porch and leave our clothes outside. Alex takes Lena to her bathroom where they shower together. I clean off in our master bathroom.

We decide the rest of the day is jammie day. We don cozy fleece pajamas and thick socks. Alex makes sandwiches and heats up some soup while Lena and I dry Mitch off and brush out his coat. After lunch, I start the fire and put on Frozen for Lena, who promptly conks out.

"I'll put her down." Alex picks our daughter up and returns a minute later. "She's out for the count. I tell you, puddle jumping is super exercise."

I'm now stretched out across all the cushions. I motion to her. "Come here."

She sways back and forth like she's deciding. Such a fucking flirt.

I pat the spot in front of me on the couch. Purse my lips.

"Fine." She rolls her eyes and sits on the very edge and arches her neck to look at me.

With one finger, I trace the side of her cheek down her nape. Goosebumps break out and she shivers. "Do you like that, Poppy?"

"I do," she whispers.

I band my arm around her midsection and guide her to lie down next to me. We press our cheeks together. I dip my face and use the top of my nose to skim her jawline and chin. She turns fully toward me and grips both sides of my neck. "I got cleared."

"I'm aware." I nibble on her lower lip and then consume her lips in a kiss. The tips of our tongues touch and wrestle a bit. We get a little lost in our make-out sesh. For the first time in forever, it feels like.

When I lift up the hem of her shirt, she grips my wrist. "I haven't got my period back yet, but I can still get pregnant. I went off birth control before the operation so we could get an idea of my hormone levels. Well, and to give us the best chance at conceiving."

"I know all of this. You don't need to stress, all of this is up to you, Poppy." I span my palm across her flat stomach. Flick my eyes across narrow scars from the surgery. Search her blue eyes for any sign of trepidation.

She blinks at me. "What I'm learning to trust throughout this experience is what you always promised me. Our love is limitless. Together, anything is possible. We'll overcome every obstacle. We'll embrace everything we create. Adopting Lena was spontaneous, but the best thing that's ever happened to me. To us. Imagine if we could give her a brother or a sister?"

"I'd love that." My finger traces one of the healed laparoscopy scars that's just above her waistband. "As long as you're ready."

"I'm down an ovary and fallopian tube, the odds of me getting pregnant are not high. Dr. Madison said that if I don't conceive after six months or so, we should consider fertility drugs so I spew out all my eggs." Alex has the best way to distill serious subjects down to something that doesn't feel so, well, serious.

I push her top up and lean down and kiss the three little scars on her belly. She strokes my hair as I move lower and peel her pajama bottoms off in the process. Her familiar sweet scent of arousal permeates my nose.

When I bury my tongue in her pussy, my cock threatens to burst through the fabric of my joggers.

"Gawd, it feels amazing to have you go down on me just for pleasure and not to take away my pain," Alex moans. I'd never considered things from this perspective because, to me, every time I taste her it's gratifying for me to the nth degree.

I wiggle my tongue on her clit and lap up her cream before looking up at her from between her legs. "I don't know if I have the patience not to fuck you now, Poppy. I'm so fucking pent-up. Can we revisit the oral later tonight when we have more time?"

"Absolutely. I need you inside me. I'm already so close."

Since this is our first time having sex since her operation, I want to be gentle. Take things slow. I sit up, grab her ankles and bend her knees so her feet rest on my chest. Keeping her legs pressed together, I roll her to the side. Her pink pussy lips beckon from between her thighs. A slight shift toward her, and I'm able to guide my cock all the way inside.

Holy fucking heaven. She's so tight. So warm. So velvety.

Placing one foot on the floor for leverage, I rock into her from this sideways angle. Slowly but steadily. Watch my length disappear deep inside her and reappear glistening with her arousal.

Alex is quiet but puffs out little breaths and almost indecipherable squeaks with each thrust. Her eyes never veer from mine when she pinches her nipples with one hand and reaches up to grip my neck with the other. Her pussy squeezes me. Milks me.

I slip my hand between her legs and rub her clit, which sends her off. Her eyes squeeze shut and she bites her lip when she comes. It triggers my own release, which floods her. Quickly, I pull my T-shirt off and shove it under where we are joined so there's not a wet spot on the living room couch.

"Wow," she says dreamily as she rolls over and puts her feet up.

"Yeah, wow." I take in her odd position. "Why are you lying like that?"

"Oh, just giving your swimmers a chance to get where they're supposed to." She exaggerates the position and winks at me.

"Holy hell, did those words just come out of Alex LeRoux's mouth?" I speak in an exaggerated gossip-columnist voice and give her jazz hands.

She joins in. "You heard it here, folks. Jace Deveraux and Alex LeRoux may have just deliberately made a baby."

"I'll post it on social." I pretend to take a picture of our semi-naked bodies. She even gives me a duck face.

Hands down, Alex is my absolute favorite person.

She proves it to me over and over again.

Now that we've overcome this crisis, it's time to resume discussion of the wedding.

Because I'll be damned if anything's going to stop us now.

Chapter Thirteen

One Month Later

IT'S ANOTHER GORGEOUS DAY, unseasonably warm. I'm unable to keep still while waiting for Zoey to get here. When her Audi finally turns the corner and appears in the driveway, I can't help but bounce up and down. She's been in Los Angeles during most of my recovery, so while we've FaceTimed quite a bit, I haven't seen her in person since her wedding.

The second she parks, I yank the door off the hinges. "Get your ass out here, woman. I cannot believe you'd keep this from me."

She slides out of her car and flings herself into my arms. "Alex, you know I had to. But obviously, I'm telling you now. Well, after my parents, of course. We're due later this year and I've never been so excited."

I motion for her to follow me inside. My appetite hasn't returned since my surgery, but now that Jace and I are actively trying to get pregnant, I make sure I eat healthy food every day. When we get to the kitchen, I pull out a meat and cheese tray he made before he took Lena to the grocery store. The smell seems off.

Zoey doesn't seem to notice. She makes herself a couple of crackers and groans. "God, this is delicious. Now that I'm through my first trimester, holy hell. I'm an eating machine."

"How is Ty doing? Jace was a little bummed that the band decided to take three additional months. I think he's getting worried that LTZ is calling it quits." I pick up a piece of Brie and smell it. Seems fine.

Zoey pats her nearly flat belly. She seems to carefully think about what she's about to say. "Ty is getting anxious to go back, too. But I don't think Jace should worry. The timing makes logical sense. The restaurant opens soon. Ronni's on a three-month shoot, so when that's over, Connor should have better flexibility. I'll be huge by the time they start recording, most likely."

"I'm looking forward to all of that. Your baby bump. Recording." I take a nibble of the cheese. Then another.

"Speaking of Jace, where is he? Where's my goddaughter?"

"They're out at the grocery store getting the fixings for a peanut butter pie. It's equally annoying and equally adorable. They make pies." I make a show of rolling my eyes, but the truth is, it's seriously the cutest thing ever. "My mom taught him and he's teaching her."

Zoey laughs until she snorts. "So, the sexy drummer from LTZ is making pies. The hot singer knocked up his wife. What happened to the bad-boy rockers we picked out at The Mission?"

I wag my finger at her. "I'd bet Ty still has an eight-pack just like Jace. They were workout buddies for a long time."

Zoey's face drops briefly until she pastes on a smile. "It's true. Ty's in the gym all the time. Sometimes he works out for three hours a day." She takes the empty plate to the sink and rinses it off.

"Why?" I'm genuinely surprised. Although it kind of makes sense. Trading one addiction for another and all that.

Zoey shrugs and plays it off. "Who knows? So are you going to show me the new horses? I'm dying here."

Interesting. I expected her to unload on me today. From what Jace and the guys have been talking about, clearly something's up with Ty again. I guess it's to be expected because his mother died horrifically only a week or so before he married my bestie. During their meetings about when to resume band business, apparently, he's been very distracted and even agitated. I don't say this to Zoey, but the rest of the guys are all worried about the future of LTZ. No one's sure if Ty actually wants to keep the band going. Or is capable of it. Especially now that Zoey's pregnant.

As curious as I am to get the inside scoop, I'm proud of Zoey and I'm going to respect her decision to keep Ty's business private. It's what Jace and I always hoped for because it's the right thing for them to do as a couple. When they initially got back together, he and I would get dragged into their juvenile drama on so many occasions. Almost like they were emotionally frozen in time at the young age they broke up.

It's a relief that they've gotten over that hump, so I don't mind if that part of our relationship has changed. As we make the short trek to the barn, I ask, "So, how does it feel?"

"Being pregnant? Kind of weird. A little abstract. Nothing much to report yet." She pats King on his neck and kisses his cheek. "You're the one with the craziness going on. How are you holding up? I'm glad your cramps finally stopped."

"Thank gawd." I grab a bunch of carrots and give one to Samantha. I can't help but give her a little attention, she's such a great horse. The liberty training has bonded us immensely.

When I glance over at Zoey, she's looking at me with a heart full of sisterhood. "I've never seen you happier. I'm so glad you have Jace and Helena. And this beautiful property. I love you. I love all of this for you."

We spend a bit of time grooming the horses and gossiping about Ronni and Fiona before heading back to the house so Zoey can see Jace and Lena. We find them working hard on a pie. I nearly burst into tears, because I scrubbed every inch of the kitchen and it's now destroyed. Flour. Sugar. Pie dough. Shortening. Peanut Butter. It looks like they had a food fight. Zoey gasps. Her hands fly up to cover her mouth.

I, too, must appear shell-shocked, because Jace has the decency to look embarrassed. "We'll clean it up, don't worry."

"Mama, we make pee-butt pie!" Lena runs up to me covered in flour and sugar from head to toe and almost gets her arms around me.

"I can see that, so keep the grubby little mitts off me until your dad cleans you and this kitchen up." I decide to let it go and trust Jace to handle things. He always does. Doesn't mean I'm going to stay in here and look at the mess. "We're going to sit out under the heater on the porch, babe."

"Thank you, Jesus. I seem to always be freezing. This pregnancy hormone thing is whack. You sure you don't want to get yourself married and knocked up too?" Zoey grabs a couple of blankets from the couch for us on our way back outside.

I turn the heaters on, and we curl up on the porch swing. "Married? Yeah. Probably soon. Knocked up? Not a chance. We're not planning for other kids."

As we chat about the foundation and my certification process, in the back of my mind, I'm wondering why I flat-out lied to Zoey about our plan to try for a baby. I think it's because part of me doesn't want to get her hopes up.

Or mine.

Zoey doesn't notice my inner struggle, thank gawd. "Part of me thought you'd change your mind after Lena and the surgery. Especially once I got pregnant. But I get it. You've always known what you want."

If only that were true. Strangely, cold pricks start to dance down my spine. I feel insanely woozy and nauseated. A dull ache spreads in my lower belly, which puts me on hyper-alert. I'm trying to focus and catalog what's going on in my body. I keep my gaze fixed on the pasture but still attempt to listen to what Zoey's saying. When the prickles turn into a full-blown chill, I can't stop the full-body shudder. Instinctively, I tighten my blanket around me.

"Is everything okay?" Zoey scoots over to me and grips my shoulder. "You're super pale."

I try to concentrate on her question. "Uh, yeah. Of course, I just miss this. Whenever you and I have time together, it makes me realize how little we see each other anymore."

"Adulting is weird. Of course, having a lot of sex with the guys we love is definitely not weird. It's awesome. I'd never want to go back to being eighteen." She shudders.

"Hell, no." I overenthusiastically agree. I keep trying to pay attention and participate, but I'm feeling super weak. My voice comes out all weird and a little high-pitched. "Are you guys going to the friends-and-family opening for Fiona's restaurant?"

She looks at me like I've lost my mind. "Of course. It would be hard for the band to play without Ty. Do you really think the guys will be able to pull off a secret show at The Mission? Ty told me the guys are coming out here for a weekend to rehearse."

"They are? I didn't know about it." I'm super discombobulated all of a sudden.

Zoey's grips my hand. "Um, I didn't realize…"

In this moment, all I want is to get inside without worrying Zoey. She'll understand. I'll explain it later. Except, when I stand up, I'm faint. I feel blood pooling in the maxi-pad I put on this morning. Just in case. It's soaked it through for sure. I know I'm acting super weird, but I have to take care of it.

"Are you sure you're okay?" Zoey reaches over to feel my forehead. Clearly, she's not fooled.

"I'm fine," I mumble some excuse about not eating and needing to talk to Jace and leave her on the porch.

Jace looks up from the book he's reading Lena when I burst through the door. I put my finger to my lips and motion for him to follow me to the kitchen, which is now spotless. Quickly, he's up and by my side. "What's going on, Poppy? You're white as a ghost."

"I'm pretty sure I got my period. Can you get Lena's coat? I'll have Zoey watch her so you can help me without prying little eyes."

He nods but gives me a side-eye. A few minutes later, I carry my darling daughter out and plop her down next to Zoey on the porch. I give my bestie the look that only BFFs can get away with. "Lena, will you show Zoey the chickens?"

Zoey glances up at me, takes the hint and turns her attention to Lena. The smile that threatens to fly off her face gives me relief. Thank gawd she's psyched to have one-on-one time with her goddaughter. By the time I get back inside, Jace has the shower running for me. I drop the blanket I've kept wrapped around me and strip out of my clothes. Sure enough, my jeans and panties look like a murder scene. Jace is aghast. "Poppy, this isn't normal."

"Dr. Madison told me my period would be delayed after surgery and that it would be heavier, but holy hell. I wasn't expecting this. No wonder I feel woozy, I've lost a ton of blood in a short period of time." I roll up my ruined jeans and underwear into a ball. "Can you toss these for me while I rinse off?"

"I'll be back in a sec; I'm not leaving you alone like this." He disappears and is back literally fifteen seconds later to find me cleaning myself off in the shower.

That's when I notice Jace still has pie dough in his hair and on his neck. I can't help but point and laugh. He looks in the mirror and back at me. Cocks an eyebrow. "Don't try to deflect. I'm worried."

"I'm sure it's fine," I try to reassure him. "I'll double up the pads, throw on some sweats, and go tell Zoey what's happening. She'll understand."

Except, I immediately soak through two extra-absorbent overnight pads in succession. I call Dr. Madison's emergency line while Jace runs outside to find Zoey and fetch our daughter. Thankfully, Jen and Becca are only five minutes away from home. The second they arrive, Jace and I head to the emergency room.

I'm freaking the fuck out.

For the life of me, I can't understand it when doctors assure you something is normal when every bone in your body knows it's not.

All I can do is remain calm. Or try, anyway.

If there's anything I've learned during this shit-show of a health journey?

Control is just an illusion.

Chapter Fourteen

A Couple of Weeks Later

Miscarriage.

What weird terminology. I mean, I get it. Alex was technically carrying an embryo that didn't take. It just seems like such a cold term. Clinical. We didn't, for a moment, consider she might be pregnant when she started bleeding.

Well, sure. We're reasonably intelligent adults. There was always a chance when we started having unprotected sex. But seriously? It was miniscule. Alex lost half her reproductive organs. She hadn't gotten her period back yet.

It took Ty and Zoey months to conceive. For us? A couple of weeks.

Alex and I truly believed we'd fuck with abandon and when she wasn't able to get pregnant, she'd go on Clomid and we'd end up with octuplets. It was a joke we shared every time she propped her legs up on the pillows at just the right angle to make sure my sperm got to where it needed to be. We even named them hippie-dippie off-the-grid names. River. Stream. Tree. Seashell. Wind. Pebble. Twiggy. And Jeff.

Because isn't there always a Jeff?

"Okay, babe, I'm going into the city to see Zoey and Fiona." Alex is twinning with Lena. Both wear white t-shirts, olive cargo pants and denim jackets and, of course, black Frye boots. "I hope you enjoy some time to yourself."

I kiss them goodbye and head up to the practice space. I've been working on building drumming strength back up. It's a strenuous, athletic gig and with LTZ playing Fiona's restaurant opening, I've got to be on my "A" game.

A couple hours later, after I shower and dress in nondescript clothes, I drive to Jake's Pickup for an awesome roast beef sandwich on homemade bread. It's a nice-enough day, so I decide to take it down to the beach and catch up on some calls.

First up is my dad. My folks just returned from an extended visit to Sweden and Norway and I'm grateful he's back. "Pops, you're home. How was the trip?"

"Have you not seen all the pictures I posted on Facebook?" He loves to joke with me about a skill set he doesn't understand. "Aren't you supposed to be some sort of social media guru?"

I click on FaceTime and soon his face fills my screen. He's grown out his hair, it's nearly to his shoulders. "Look at you trying to copy your son's long hair. Doesn't Sweden have any barbers? In answer to your question, Facebook is very 2011."

"Eh? Who has time for that anyway? Yeah, so, I thought I'd throw caution to the wind and forget about haircuts. I like it." He gives me a cheesy smile and moves the phone in close so I can only see his teeth.

"Don't tell me, you got a tattoo and a piercing too."

He laughs. Then his face grows serious. "Enough. How are the two of you holding up? I know you insisted we not cut our trip short, but it was all I could do to stop your mom from booking flights home."

"We're doing okay. Alex seems to be taking it in stride after all her body's been through. Her doctor assured us that we could still keep on trying." I don't tell him that Alex missed her period again this month. We're waiting a couple of weeks for her to take a pregnancy test. From everything her doctor told us, her body's still healing, so we're trying to keep our minds clinical and not emotional.

It's not easy for me. Or her.

Pops scrubs his scruffy chin with his hand. "Look, it's none of my business, but if the band is picking back up again, is now the best time to be trying for a baby?"

"Well, endometriosis isn't ever cured. They got most of it, but the chances of it reoccurring are fairly high if she's not on some hormonal therapy. We want to try now so Lena has a brother or sister close to her age. Then we can decide what protocol is best to keep Alex healthy in the long-run." The words tumble out of my mouth. Jen and Becca know what's going on, but we don't go into this many details with them. Alex and I have great communication skills, but we both believe in privacy. So, I haven't talked to anyone but her during all of this.

The picture on his phone gets a little blurry as he moves through the house, then he comes back into focus. He's sitting in the kitchen. My mom is puttering around behind him. "Makes sense."

"Plus, I don't think there's ever a right time."

"That's true. So, any movement on the wedding? Your mom invited all of Sweden and Norway over for the big occasion."

"Nope."

"Here's an idea. Maybe tag onto Jen's. Save a few bucks." He puts on his glasses and peers back into the screen.

I shake my head. "With all that's going on, we haven't even talked about it. It will happen when it happens."

"Just don't elope in Vegas, I'd have to disown you." He chuckles.

"Ah, well. Good thing I don't need your blood money. I can pay for my own wedding. So could Alex, you know." I point and jab at the phone.

Mom comes up behind him. "My only son, if you elope I'll kill you after he disowns you. I've been waiting for you kids to get married. To have a proper wedding. Don't take away the one thing I've been looking forward to."

"My only mom. If that's the one thing you've been looking forward to, I'm feeling extraordinarily sorry for you right now." She makes a pouty face. "Stop, I promise we won't elope in Vegas."

"Okay then."

They fill me in on the trip and what's going on with Jaylynn and we wrap it up.

While I was on the phone, I see that Alex sent me and the rest of the guys a picture of all the girls throwing rock horns, including Lena and Mia. Various texts from the guys and Ronni follow. It gets me thinking. On a whim, I dial Zane's number.

"My dude?" He picks up on the first ring. "What's wrong?"

I accept his FaceTime request. "Uh, nothing?"

"During our downtime, you never just call," Zane admonishes.

I think about it for a minute. Realize it's true and shouldn't be. "Well, I'll jump in then. I'm wondering how you're feeling about the band. Connor's got his hands full and doesn't even live in Seattle anymore. Something's going on with Ty again. You and I seem to have our shit locked down. I guess I was wondering if you have a backup plan. I love being out here on the ranch, but at some point, I'd like to have even a short tour to look forward to."

"Oh, I feel ya." He looks off into the distance. "The Mission is cool and all, but it's not my dream. Gus is taking all of Fee's time in the months leading to this opening. I rarely see her. I'm basically a house husband. Not that there's anything wrong with it, but I'm getting antsy. We're almost five months into year two of our hiatus."

"From a marketing perspective, I'm trying to be realistic. I think we have a window, but if we let it go much further we might not get back to where we were." I blow out a huge breath. One I've been holding for months. We've been so consumed with Alex's health, I haven't allowed myself to think about what I want. Which is my band.

"We should have a meeting. Maybe even fly to Connor if we have to."

"Yeah, and that brings up something else. We need to decide on management. Katherine's upset that we blew off her schedule, but I think she'll always push us in the direction that isn't who we are as a band anymore."

Zane nods. "Yeah, I agree. I'm not happy with how they exploited Ty all those years. I'm mad at myself for everything that happened with Andrew and Sienna. Part of me wonders if Ty's reluctance to commit to anything is because he doesn't want to relive all that shit."

"I never thought about it from that point of view." Zane is like Ty's brother, so I value his opinion. Even if he'll always protect Ty. I care deeply about our singer, but so much of what went down took a personal toll on me too. It's not all Ty's fault though. I've been thinking if I can take some personal responsibility, maybe I can get rid of the resentment that's built up during our hiatus.

Huh. Resentment.

Zane leans back in his chair and holds the phone up at an angle. "Ty's seeing Lisa regularly again. In my opinion, that's why he's a little fucked up. Dredging up the past and shit."

"I've got to ask, is he drinking? Or is it coke again?" I can't help but furrow my brow. If he started down the substance abuse path again, I think that would be it for me.

"No, I don't think so. He said he's trying to get closure from his mother's death. He's never lived a very traditional life; I'm guessing he's also just trying to settle into the prospect of being a father when the only father figure he ever had was Carter." For a man with the knob turned to eleven all the fucking time, I'm always astounded by how insightful Zane is. "It's tough because we really aren't LTZ without any one of us. I wouldn't be into carrying on the band if one of us left."

"Me either."

"The thing is, even though we've written a couple new songs for LTZ, Ty still gets his music fix from producing artists. He and Connor just finished mastering Fireball's album. He's also working with some acts from his foundation. Connor has some extra stuff going on too. Did you know he had a role in Ronni's Netflix show?"

My jaw drops open. I shut it right away before anyone notices. Zane's revelation astounds me. I can't believe Connor never said anything. "So, Connor's going to be an actor now?"

"Nah, nothing like that." Zane waves me off. "He's a background character. Ronni did it as a way to keep the twins on set. The network even sprung for daycare. Connor's role in taking down Kircher made him a hot commodity."

"Wow. I was so caught up in Zoey's accident and the aftermath with Sienna, I keep forgetting about that. Ronni is such a fucking badass."

Zane raises an eyebrow. "When you think about it, LTZ has been through the ringer on all fronts."

It occurs to me that the three other guys have been in constant communication about their lives while I've basically blown them off this entire year. They're my brothers. My best friends. I can do better. I will do better. "We have been through the shit, that's for sure. So, um, apparently you and I are the loyalists, but how would you feel about jamming with some musician friends, just for fun?"

"What do you think?" He winks at me.

"I'll talk to Alex about it, but the idea is fucking awesome. It would be fun to do something experimental. Nothing we have to worry about getting on the radio." I feel the germination of excitement at being creative again. "Meanwhile, let's think about putting together another band meeting. One where Connor is here to participate. I'd like to get some clarity on what our plans are one way or the other."

"Yup. Me too. I'm not ready for LTZ to be over, though. Just putting it out there." Zane pinches the upper part of his nose.

"Me either, my brother."

After we wrap up the call, I decide to head back home. I pull out my laptop and log into my coursework for the Institute of Human-Animal Connection. Before we adopted Lena, Alex and I planned to use LTZ's year off to get our certifications and get her horse therapy business up and running. Despite all good intentions, we started on it, but our timing went out the window with a toddler in the house.

Alex's health hasn't made it easy to pick it back up again either.

As I scroll through my reading materials, I wonder whether it's still our dream. Or even Alex's dream. She loves our horses, but I'm not sure how all of this is going to come together. With the band. And the rescue. It's important work. It would be a shame to give up on it.

I can't help but feel a little down on myself.

Catching up with my pops and Zane has given me some things to think about. Things that were already gnawing at me. I'll admit, I feel uncomfortably unsettled. Unsure of which way my life is going. For the first time in my adult life.

The only thing that seems permanent is my family. Lena & Alex.

What's up in the air is everything with the band.

It's not a great feeling to wonder if we're still on the same page.

Not at all.

Chapter Fifteen

Two Months Later

JACE IS HOLED AWAY in the practice room playing drums again. My dad took Lena for ice cream. Jen and Becca are away on vacation. Zoey isn't picking up the phone. Mom is out with friends. The horses have been fed and exercised. All the pets are fine and out doing their thing.

Leaving me alone for a change. Struggling with my thoughts.

I'm trying to keep things "Fonzie," as Zoey's dad always says. Somehow the phrase that Zoey and I picked up as little girls from him has permeated the entire LTZ world. I mean, none of us are old enough to be familiar with this Fonzie character. All I remember is he's a guy in a leather coat who always keeps a cool head.

Anyway, I'd love to think I'm a natural Fonzie. I like to go with the flow. My current problem is the flow I'm being forced to go with sucks.

Big time.

It's not really a flow at all, truth be told.

There's just too many things up in the air. I used to thrive on uncertainty. The idea that you can go where the wind blows whenever you want. I lived that way for many years when I was flitting all over the world as a social media travel influencer.

I was very successful. It made me rich. It also gave me many treasured memories. Falling in love with Jace is, hands-down, the best thing that's ever happened to me.

We created our own flow.

Our flow hasn't always been smooth. It slowed to a trickle during all the paternity bullshit. When we adopted Lena, it steadied and took on a life of its own. I truly believe navigating my endometriosis and miscarriages as well as we have has been possible because of our flow.

Why, then, am I so scared about our flow moving in opposite directions? It's shocking to me that I feel this way. A couple of months ago, I believed we were in perfect sync.

I think, for me, I've held myself back because I knew he'd eventually leave again. LTZ is likely going to make a huge return to the music world. They'll record an album, release it and tour. If the music connects with the listeners—and it will—Jace's obligations to the band will take over our lives.

At the exact time he and I are trying to have a viable pregnancy.

Who knew I'd be so fertile? Even with half my parts. My body is just not cooperating in letting the embryo implant itself and grow into a baby. Dr. Madison seems to believe I can get there, but after losing three pregnancies, it's starting to take an emotional toll on both of us.

I'm wondering if it's worth it.

Jace bops down the stairs mopping his forehead with a hand towel. "Hey, did you take a look at the bus mock-ups?"

"Not yet." I flick through some messages on my phone. "I trust you to configure it. It's not like I'm going to be able to be out on the road for an entire tour. Especially if we have an infant."

His face falls. "The idea is each of us will travel in a customized tour bus with our families. I need your input to make sure we have what we need. It's ours forever, so I want us to design it together."

"Jace, have you guys even decided on a management company? It seems like you're putting the cart before the horse."

He goes to the fridge and grabs a carton of milk and pours a glass. Drinks it in one gulp. "I guess you're right. We're supposed to hammer all that out next weekend at Ty's while you're at Zoey's shower."

"Hey, I'm not trying to be difficult. I think it's sweet that you want me to be with you. But Fee and I..."

"Yeah, yeah." He circles his finger in the air. "She has the restaurant and you have the horse rescue. You told me about the conversation you two had."

"Are you going to tell me what's going on with you?" I cross my arms and glare at him. "What did I do to make you so snippy with me?"

"It's not you, Poppy. I'm just feeling like our life is a little out of control, and I don't do well with it." He sits at the table in the breakfast nook and slumps over. "I'm sad we lost another baby. I'm sad that the band can't make a decision. But what makes me saddest is that at some point soon, I might be without my girls for weeks at a time and we still haven't even discussed getting married."

I sit and take his hands in mine. "I'm feeling out of sorts too. I hate that my body is failing us. I hate that we have no idea what's up with the band. I'm also scared to get pregnant again, but I'm more scared of not trying."

"I don't want to lose another one." Tears well up in his eyes. "It's so hard on you. You're bleeding. Hormonal. Do you think we should call it a day?"

When Jace cries, which is rare, I can't help but join him. Tears stream down my face. "Dr. Madison still feels we have a chance."

"I can't help but wonder if the risks you're taking are worth it. If we want kids, there are plenty of ways to make that happen. I mean, you've made your brand on rescuing animals. Maybe..." He looks up at me, questioning.

I nod. "I've thought about it. Can we give it another shot before we start going down that path?"

"Of course. If you're up for it." We clutch each other's hands tightly across the table.

"As for LTZ, you already spoke with Zane. Hopefully, things will be cleared up this weekend when Connor and Ronni arrive." I knee him under the table. "Take control and force them to make some sort of decision. One way or another, something needs to move forward. Stagnation is evil."

This elicits a smirk, signifying the Jace I know and love is back in the building.

For now.

I guess we'll see what next weekend brings.

On the ferry ride over to Seattle, Jace informs me of a little detail I hadn't been aware of.

"So, let me get this straight," I say to him on the drive to Ty and Zoey's after I've had a chance to digest. "The day you sent Zoey home when I was bleeding, she now thinks I was pretending not to feel well and that I was mad at you because the guys were coming out to the ranch to rehearse?"

Jace grits his teeth. "Uh, yeah?"

"Um... How in the world did you think that would fly?"

He shrugs. "I mean, in my defense, I was scared out of my mind and not thinking straight. All I knew is you were frickin' bleeding and you hadn't told her we were trying for a baby. I might have panicked. I'm not the best liar, you know."

"So, wait, does Zoey still think you're all going to Poulsbo for the night?"

"Um... Yeah?"

"Ohmygawd. How are you going to explain why we're driving in together?" I shake my head and laugh.

He looks over at me, his eyebrows raised. "Fuck, I didn't even think..."

"And where is Ty?" I'm stunned at how inept these guys are when they have to plan things for themselves, but it doesn't stop me from laughing at Jace. "Rookie mistakes, I tell you."

"I don't know! I posted a bunch of pictures and took funny videos, Poppy." He's laughing so hard he's heaving. "I didn't handle diversionary logistics."

"Clearly. Pull over and let's switch sides. When we drive through the gate, duck down. Once we're through, you can jump out and hide until we leave for our walk. Gawd. What would you do without me?"

He wipes his eyes and clutches his flat belly. "I'm never planning on finding out.

Minutes later, our caper works. Jace is safely hiding behind a bush. For all I know, Ty's in the bushes too.

Taking a deep breath to mentally prepare myself, I push the door open and give, what I hope, is the appropriate level of enthusiasm for my future godchild. I can't help but rub Zoey's belly. "Holy shit, Z. Look at this! Have you really been impregnated by the lead singer of LTZ?"

"Do you think he'll notice me if I have his baby?" Zoey playfully juts out her hip and twirls her hair.

I bite my lip and try to course correct the stupid lie the boys told. "I'm sorry about when you were over. I should have just told you I wasn't feeling well. You just came all that way."

"It's all good. Is everything okay now?"

"It's all fine, just some hormone adjustments. I haven't wanted to bog you down with it because of your little man in there." I can't stop myself from touching her again. "Can we talk about it later, though? Fiona texted me. She wanted us to pop over to her house for some appetizer she's testing out. I'm kinda hungry, and, well, it's Fee. Should we go?"

Zoey grabs a jacket and we set off. I wink at Jace when we pass. Luckily, she doesn't even notice. "I'm supposed to walk thirty minutes a day. Can we take the scenic route so I get my exercise in?"

I text Fee to let her know what's up. Zoey and I keep the conversation light as we weave through the mansions in her neighborhood. When we approach Fee's house, it's clear she's gone all out for this shower. The dead giveaway is the blue balloon explosion. She has literally every shade I can imagine lining their walkway leading up to a fifteen-foot arch. "Surprise!" I jump up and down and clap my hands. "We fooled you!"

I'm surprised by how emotional I feel. It doesn't help that Zoey sobs unabashedly. She's so touched. As she should be. Our friends are incredible. They've all shown up for Zoey. So have all the moms. Fee's outdone herself. The cake is amazing. The food's world class. It's a wonderful way to welcome Zoey to the fold.

Ronni stands and uses her spoon to tap on her glass. "Zoey, on behalf of all of us here, we welcome you to the mother club. It's an experience like no other."

"Absolutely. And to your third trimester. Heartburn, constipation, giant tits, and the inability to ever get comfortable," Fiona toasts.

We banter and joke and tell stories. The entire afternoon is one big TMI. All I can think about is how much I want to confide my fertility journey to all of these fabulous women. Tell them about what I've been through. I'm not sure why I've been so closed off because they'd embrace me. Support me. Be there for me.

I do know that Zoey's baby shower isn't the appropriate time to share I've had two miscarriages. "Enough of the sappy shit. Presents. Now."

Zoey stands and plunks back down. She looks uncomfortable and flushed. I have flashbacks to the award show when she spent the evening in the bathroom. She recovers quickly, and we all move into the living room.

Her mom helps her to the couch. "Once that belly pops, the discomfort starts. Get used to it."

Tiny, gorgeous Ronni, who looks like she's never even thought of having a baby let alone birthing twins, laments, "You should have seen my belly when I hit five months. I never thought I'd look skinny again. Well, I don't, but man. I was twice your size. The twins, God love them, have fucked up my body big time."

I chime in, and I cannot believe the words out of my mouth. "You're gorgeous, Ronni. But, to your point, I can't say I'm envious. I didn't have to go through any of that shit and I have a beautiful daughter."

Fuck me. Defensive much?

I sound like such a demented bitch. I'm hiding the truth. I'm so fucking ashamed of myself. Luckily, no one seems to notice. I guess they're used to my insensitive comments about pregnancy. It's hard for me to concentrate for the rest of the shower. I manage to smile and nod at the appropriate moments until it's time to go back to Zoey's house. Her mom and I help her take the smaller bags and boxes on the short walk home.

It's painfully clear she's in distress. Cramping. I know exactly what she feels like because I've been there so many times. When we get her settled on the couch in her living room, I run downstairs to the studio.

I grip Ty's bicep and squeeze gently. Careful to keep my voice calm. "Ty, Zoey's having some cramps. Don't freak out, she's probably fine, but you should take her to the hospital to be sure."

"Fuck." Ty's face goes pale. "Okay. I'll go take care of her."

After he disappears up the stairs, Jace wraps his arms around me. "Is she okay?"

I burst into tears. "Gawd, I hope so. I really hope so."

Zane and Connor look at me like I've grown a third head.

"Uh, Alex, do you need anything?" Connor's deep voice is tinged with an Irish lilt. "Are you okay?"

"I am. We just had such a beautiful day." I sniff. "Jace, there's nothing we'll be able to do here. I want to get home to Lena. Zoey will text me from the hospital."

We say quick goodbyes. Ty, Zoey, and her mom are gone by the time we get upstairs, so we just leave.

"Poppy, tell me the truth. What's going on?"

I gaze out the window. Decide to tell the truth. "Everyone thinks my endometriosis is in the past. I'm regretting not being truthful. I regret that I'm still letting them think I don't want any more kids. Going through all of this with you, gawd. You couldn't be a better partner. Truly. But so much of being a woman is about all these changes our bodies go through. I wish I could just talk to them. I'm being so stupid."

He reaches over and grabs my hand. "Poppy, they love you. They'll understand."

I nod. But I don't agree. "You don't think it's going to be weird if they somehow find out? Realize I didn't bother to tell them about what my body's gone through? Zoey's going to be devastated that I didn't tell her. She would have wanted to hold my hand if you couldn't be there."

"Well, I was there. I know I was a bit overprotective about you talking to them, uh, before. I'm over it, though. If you want to confide in them, don't let me stop you."

"Yeah, well, thank you so much for permission. Because if something goes wrong when you're out on the road? I'll be alone again," I blurt out.

He looks over at me and doesn't say anything. His set jaw and sorrowful eyes say it all.

I hurt him.

What do I do? Nothing. I turn and look back out the window.

I guess tomorrow's a new day.

I'll just have to try to do better.

Chapter Sixteen

One Month later

WELL, THE DAY HAS finally come. Fiona's restaurant, Gus, is making its debut.

We'll play the afterparty at the renovated Mission, which is where we're getting set up for our rehearsal. Alex is with the girls over at the restaurant. Things have been a bit strained between us. All her little comments about me being gone with the band? They piss me off, but I bite my tongue. I don't want to upset her. I think showing her that things are not what she thinks rather than trying to preemptively defend myself is going to be the right way to handle things.

So, for now, I just let it go.

Zane, Connor, and I are up on stage surveying the room as our gear is being loaded off the truck. Various people mill about. Our roadies. The club's techies. Some of the staff who are setting up the bar. A bunch of musical artists from Ty's foundation sit on the floor, gaping at us.

Connor scans the room, which is state of the art. "This is fantastic, Zane, so it is. But where the fuck is Ty?"

"He's still in the car talking to Zoey. She's not been feeling well, I'm sure he'll be here in a few minutes." Zane sets his precious Gibson on its stand.

We chat about gear until Ty saunters in with perfect rock-star swagger five minutes later. "My brothers. I'm so fucking excited. I'm ready to go."

"While the gear's getting set up, let's have a quick meeting." I shove my drumsticks in my back pocket. "We're all together, and it's time we finalize some stuff with the band."

The four of us head to the green room, which is a million times better than the one at the original Mission venue we made our debut in. It's clean, for one thing.

But also like a real touring venue. Complete with a flat screen, oversized couch, and catering area.

We pull chairs into a circle. I begin, "Isis Management. Discuss."

"I'm on board, they've been feckin' great for my wee brothers' band." Connor taps his fingers on his long leg.

"So, Katherine is out?" Zane looks at each of us one by one.

"She's pressuring us to do all the things that burned us out over the years. We're not kids starting out anymore. It feels like the time is just right to make a change." Ty crosses his arms. "After all, we're all family men, or soon-to-be family men now."

"Yeah, but I still want to play. And tour." I rest my elbows on my knees and clasp my hands in front of me. "Are we all up for that?"

"If we each have our own bus, I'm cool." Connor slouches down in his seat. "You don't want to be woken up by my evil twins. Trust me."

Ty's smile spreads across his face. "Yeah, and we'll have our tiny little guy."

"Ty and I have written some songs. I know we've all been working in smaller groups, but it's time to get into the studio and work it all out." Zane points at Ty. "Last fall at your house, when you showed us the new gear, Jace joked that we should record at your house. Honestly, I think it's a cool idea. It would be the least disruptive to our families in the short-term."

Connor nods. "Aye, Ronni and I have decided to buy a place up here. Now that she's doing creative work, LA isn't where we want to raise kids. We're gonna keep our house there, of course, but we're thinking home base will be Seattle."

"Seriously?" I can't help but blurt out. "That makes me feel a million times better."

Everyone looks at me. "Were you feeling bad?" Ty's brow furrows.

"Nah, not bad. Just a bit worried that our logistics are so much more complicated now. It's been a slog to even get us to this point," I try to explain.

"We'll be fine. It's us. LTZ forever." Zane throws his fist in the air.

All of us chuckle and halfheartedly throw our fists in the air too. More in a mocking way than a brotherly way. I mean, Zane is truly something else.

"Are we all up for a quick trip to LA to meet with Isis?" I throw it out there. "I don't want to decide this via Zoom. I need the vibe."

Everyone nods. "Absolutely," Zane and Ty say in unison.

Zane adds, "Let's take the jet at the end of the week. They're chomping at the bit to work with us. I want to get this sorted before Katherine gets wind of us leaving. Even if we're parting ways, let's do it professionally. For all of the bad things that went down, there was way more positivity."

With the future of LTZ nearly buttoned up, we take five until we're ready to go through the set. Ty works on the set list. Zane pops in to check on Fee, Connor's on the phone to Ronni. I'm about to call Alex when my phone lights up with her call coming in.

I pick up. "Hey, how's everything going in there?"

"Seems like everything is under control. Fee and her team have been working on it for a month. Fermenting this. Aging that. It's like clockwork. The menu looks amazing." Alex's voice sounds a bit muffled.

"Where are you?"

"I'm in the ladies' room, the coverage isn't great. I wasn't sure if it was cool for me to come in there." She's nearly whispering. "I have news."

"Tell me, we're about to start sound check."

"I'm pregnant. I took four tests this morning. We just need to cross our fingers." Her enthusiasm is not contained, even though she's being super quiet. "I'm going to have to tell the girls, I won't be able to drink all the wine tonight."

I'm so excited. And so scared. "Come over here and watch. I want to kiss the fuck out of you."

"We can make out later, it would be weird for me to leave. Fee's got us all set up at a table, we're just waiting for Zoey."

When the call ends, I feel pretty fucking awesome. Maybe all I needed was a little stability. The band seems to be on track. God, if Alex can get through the first trimester, we might even be adding to our family.

Connor's motioning to me to get up on stage. "You'll wanna have a look at your kit."

I salute him and examine the drum setup. It's not right. My long-time tech left to tour with a pop singer, so I'm down a crew member. Which sucks ass. It's down to me to make the necessary adjustments to my gear. "Well, this feels like déjà vu," I mutter to myself, recalling our last show at this club before we had roadies.

"Fucking diva." Zane chuckles, but gives me a hand until Pokey, his loyal guitar tech, waves him over.

Connor emerges from the stage right with his bass slung low against his hips. He can barely contain his own excitement. "Hey, my brothers. Feels feckin' good to be back up on stage, not gonna lie."

Ty sits on the edge, still writing our set list. He looks as happy as I've ever seen him. He's smiling like a lunatic. I can't resist kneeling beside him and flicking his cheek. "What's got you so happy?"

"Life, man." Ty's cheesy grin is almost off-putting. "It's fucking awesome."

Something about Ty's demeanor sends prickles up my neck. A weird feeling comes over me. Anxiousness, maybe. I try to mask it and be supportive. "Yeah, sure is. Hey, you forgot to include Butterfly, we should play that tonight."

Ty nods. "Yeah. We should." He scribbles it down as encore. "Good?"

"Yep." I return to the rear of the stage to finish setting up my drums and try to get the gnawing feeling of doom out of my mind. I adjust my stool, clack my sticks together, and beat out a rhythm to Down.

Connor plucks a scale of low bass notes. Zane joins in on guitar. Everything clicks into place when Ty grabs the microphone, taps it and shouts through the PA, "We're fucking back, my brothers."

"Feckin right we are," Connor answers.

For a musician, very little is better than performing. We run through our entire set to an audience of Ty's foundation kids. When we stop, all of us know that our magic is still intact.

LTZ is back, I'm going to be a father again, and I couldn't be happier. Carter shows up and he, Zane, and Ty disappear into the dressing room. While we wait for them to finish whatever it is they're doing, Connor and I sit on the edge of the stage talking to the musicians in the room.

We're interrupted by a loud crash in the dressing room, followed by the type of yelling and screaming I've never heard before. It sounds like the room is being destroyed.

Connor and I look at each other in panic, jump off the stage and run toward the dressing room.

"Pokey, keep everyone out," I scream over my shoulder. "And no fucking pictures or videos, I mean it. If I find out anyone here posts anything on social, you will never be associated with LTZ ever again."

Connor flings the door open to a horror show. Ty is like a caged animal. The look on his face is terrifying. He's pinned Carter to the ground and is pummeling him with every ounce of strength he has. The man's been a gym rat since our hiatus and is shockingly strong. Zane's no slouch himself. He's trying to pull Ty off and can't budge him.

I have no idea what to think. Ty's yelling all sorts of crazy things. "You cock-sucking motherfucker. What have you done? What have you fucking done?"

Finally, Zane is able to use his Krav Maga training to pull Ty off and put him in a headlock. I wince when he smashes Ty's face and knees him in the nose. Our singer crumples to the floor, his nose a bloody, pulpy mess. Zane's got him pinned, his fist raised and cocked when Connor and I pull him back.

Jesus. LTZ is done. There's no way to come back from this. I don't have a clue what set him off, but there's no way we can trust Ty around our families. Not after this.

No fucking way.

It doesn't even matter why he beat the shit out of Carter. It's his lack of self-control that pisses me off. Ty has none of it. I'm so fucking sad. Angry. Then it hits me. Ty's actions ruined Fee's restaurant opening.

Zane must be utterly devastated. He's in terrible shape, hovered over Carter, who is unconscious. He starts CPR, but it's his keening wails that do me in. "Wake up. Dad. Daddy."

Finally, Connor speaks. "What the actual feck? What happened?"

Zane points at Ty as he frantically does CPR on Carter. "He fucking killed Carter. You're so fucked up, Ty. Seriously. Stay the fuck away from us."

Apparently, someone had the intelligence to call 9-1-1. When the EMTs rush in, they take over CPR and get Carter stable enough to load into the ambulance. On his way out, Zane points at Ty and yells, "Fuck you."

I don't blame him.

Except Ty's not done with his destruction. He roars after him, "No, fuck you. And fuck Carter. You are both fucking dead to me."

Without thinking, I reach out to Ty and grip his arm. He whips around, hissing like a possessed man. "Don't you fucking touch me, you have no idea how sick to death I am of you treating me like a fucking child."

And with that, I'm done. I hold my hands up and walk over to Connor's side. We both watch him, transfixed. Part of me, the guy who's known Ty for over a decade, wants to get him some help.

The other part of me, the father and hopefully soon-to-be husband, is done with the man. Cemented when Ty literally growls at us and closes the coffin lid on our band. "What? Do you want a piece of me too? Have I been a big joke to all of you? All these years? Wind Ty up. Put him on stage. Use his songs. Rip his soul out. Pat him on the head. Fucking repeat. It's all fine, right? We've made our money, right? You're all rich now, right? Well fuck this. I fucking quit. There is no more LTZ. It's fucking over. If I never see any of you again it will be too fucking soon."

With that, he storms toward the loading dock. Connor and I follow him back into the main room and witness the aftermath. All of his foundation artists look horrified. Some are crying. This man represented a future to them, and he's let his demons ruin everything. "There won't be a show tonight, kids," he snarls as he passes.

Two police officers are waiting by the back door. They slam him against the wall, yank his arms behind his back and cuff him. His face is destroyed. The fight's gone out of him. His eyes are utterly blank.

Ty is an empty shell of a man. A man who just completely and totally fucked himself and seems intent on bringing all of us down with him.

Connor and I look at each other. His eyes are like saucers. I'm sure mine are too. Reality catches up to me, "I need to get to Alex."

"Feck. Let's go." He bolts toward the front door.

I feel like I have whiplash.

How did my band implode with no warning? The anger I feel toward Ty is like a powder keg that's exploded into a zillion pieces. I've kept my shit together for so many years. Held my tongue. Played my part. Mostly to keep the peace in my band and for Alex's sake. And Zoey's, for that matter.

No more.

It's time to face reality. And my reality is, I won't deliberately let any toxicity enter into mine or Alex's life. Not when we have to take care of precious cargo.

As far as I'm concerned, my band is dead. Ty's dead to me too.

That's a fact.

I may not like it, but it's my truth.

Chapter Seventeen

That Same Day

FEE LOOKS STUNNING.

She wears a tall, white chef hat. One long, pink braid drapes over her ample breasts. She's in all black, including her apron, which has the Gus logo emblazoned prominently to the left side.

Ronni and I sit at the plush chef table inside the kitchen, watching the magic happen. Fee's so cool and confident. Her brigade is dedicated. She's recruited them from the best kitchens from all over the world.

It's her dream to have Seattle's first Michelin star restaurant. I feel honored and lucky to be at the opening. She's going to make history.

We watch as she looks around the kitchen. Swoops through the cozy dining area to check that everything is perfect. She disappears into the back and returns to our table with a bottle of vintage Dom Perignon. "I thought we deserved to have a little toast with the expensive stuff. Zoey can't drink anyway, so we won't feel bad she's not here yet."

Shit. I open my mouth to say something, but nothing comes out. Fee pours us each a glass. I decide, one tiny sip won't hurt, and then I'll tell my friends I can't drink it. I mean, when will I ever get to taste this stuff again?

We clink our glasses together and each take a sip. Fiona hands us the menu. It's been years since Jace and I were in Paris and had a meal like this. I can hardly believe my dear friend is going to feed us such an amazing feast.

"O.M.G." Ronni licks her lips. "Crab with avocado, ginger lime and cucumber? No, wait. Foie gras seared with sunchoke, dates, and water chestnut? I'm going off my diet to eat this, Fee. It's going to be sooooo worth it!"

Fee beams. "I'm most proud of the duck dish. I've roasted it with ardive, which is like radicchio and Marcona almonds. I've braised it with foie gras and potato. I think the desserts are incredibly special too; I poached the sous pastry chef from Alinea. She's created this amazing fondant of maple she's braised in a bourbon barrel with milk for the past week. We're serving it with shaved ice."

"A lot of this is over my head, considering my skills are limited to heating up soup. I'm looking forward to such a well-thought-out feast, Fee. Bravo." I raise my champagne glass again to toast her awesomeness, even though I'm not having a second sip. As we clink glasses, I'm about to confide about my fertility situation and possible pregnancy when we hear an enormous crash from inside The Mission.

In a flash, Fiona bolts to the back. We follow close behind through the kitchen to a closet-sized room off the dish pit. Her ear is pressed to what looks to be a long, skinny panel in the wall. "This is a secret door to the green room. We're planning on using it for catering big shows."

The three of join her at the weird little door and press our ears to it too. I notice a nearly invisible keyhole with a button. "Fuck." Fiona angrily pounds on the door. "Zane has the master key. We haven't gotten copies made yet."

She pulls her phone out of her apron and calls, presumably, Zane. There's no answer. She shoves it back in the pouch. "Can either one of you ladies call your man? I don't want to make a big scene by going through the front door, but it's kinda crucial for me to know what's going on."

I try Jace. Ronni tries Connor. No answer from either of them.

"Fuck." She turns to leave when we hear Ty yelling. Well, not just yelling, screaming obscenities at the top of his lungs. Followed by the excruciating sounds of a terrible and violent fight. Zane's roaring down the place. There's more fighting.

We're all paralyzed in fear. Fee's dishwashing staff stare at us with wide eyes.

"Gather everyone into the staff lounge. Stay there until I say otherwise," she directs, surprisingly calm under what must be overwhelming pressure. Immediately, her employees do as she asks.

"What the fuck is happening?" Ronni shrieks when we hear Connor yelling.

We run through the restaurant out the front and to the entrance of The Mission. It's also locked, and the box office staff are nowhere to be found. We can hear sirens in the distance. A bunch of them. Fear takes root at the base of my spine.

"Fuck!" Fiona yells and starts pacing and banging on the door. "I should have never given my fucking keys to Zane. I'm going up to the office, at least I have backups for this door. Thank Christ there's not a line yet."

As she runs back to the restaurant, my phone buzzes. I look down and see that I missed a call from Zoey. I shoot her a quick text:

Hurry.

What's going on?

I'm not quite sure, but the band are all yelling at each other. The door is locked, Ronni and I can't get in there.

I'll text Ty.

As the sirens approach and five cop cars and a couple of ambulances peel into the side parking lot adjacent to the club, the voices get louder. And angrier. We can't see the load-in dock from where we're standing at the foyer, but we decide to stay put.

My phone buzzes again, this time I pick up.

"Dude? What's going on?" Zoey sounds panicked.

I'm still out of breath from our sprint. "I'm trying to listen, but I can't hear a thing other than yelling."

"Wait, what? Have you talked to Jace?"

I have to shush her so I can hear. "One second. Uh, shit. There's shouting. It's super loud. Sounds like Ty.

Hold on I think the door's opening. Nope. Oh...yeah it's opening. It's Jace. Hold on, Zoey. Jace? I'm here. What's going on?"

"Fucking chaos. It's a fucking disaster." Jace and Connor burst through the front door, both of their eyes are wild. Ronni and I peer inside and can see all the way through the room. People are standing around, shell-shocked.

Connor grabs Ronni. "Come here, love. I've got you."

Jace pulls me into his arms. I cling to him in the doorway. A loud crash interrupts us. EMTs wheel Carter out to the ambulance. Zane follows, crying uncontrollably. On his way out, he kicks over another band's amp in an utter display of grief. He turns to see what crashed to the ground and wails in agony.

"Ohmygod," I scream. "Jace, get him outta there."

The four of us race through the showroom out the loading dock to get to Jace, passing Ty on our way. Officers are reading him his Miranda rights. We make it outside to see Zane sitting next to an unconscious Carter in the ambulance. He's still bawling his eyes out.

I look up at Jace, whose face is stoic. Probably from shock. I grab his hand and squeeze. He squeezes back, but his face remains impassive as he takes in the entire scene.

That's when I see Zoey, all dressed up, cupping her belly, running through the parking lot toward the building. Her security guard, Omar is on her heels. She sees us and the look on her face breaks my heart.

Utter devastation.

"Don't." Jace encircles my wrist when I make a move toward her.

I tilt my face up and kiss his scruffy chin. "I have to. None of this is her fault. I need to be there for her."

With Jace appeased, I rush over to my bestie and hug her tightly. It's up to me to prepare her for Ty's arrest. Whatever has gone down will have permanent repercussions on all of us, that much is clear. "Zoey, shhh. Calm down."

"How am I supposed to calm down? Where is my husband?" She's in absolute hysterics. "Where is he?"

Before I can tell her the little I know, Ty is led from the loading dock in handcuffs. Zoey lurches out of my embrace and rushes toward him. A police officer stops her, but she cranes her head around him and yells, "Ty. Baby?"

He looks over at her. His face has been beaten to a bloody pulp. His eyes are dead. It's like he doesn't even register that his wife is there. I watch her fall apart when he says nothing as he's shoved into the back seat of the police car and the door is slammed behind him. For one fleeting second, he glances at her through the window. Then just looks away.

Fucking asshole. Inexcusable. I run over to her and wrap my arm around her as the police car drives away.

"What is going on?" She falls to her knees, crying.

I keep my voice calm because none of us know what the fuck is up. I'm so worried about her, she's white as a ghost. "I'm trying to get to the bottom of it. You look pale, Z. Please come inside and sit down. You don't want anything to hurt the baby."

Zoey looks up at me and her body begins to go slack. "Alex, please help me. I've got to protect my baby..." She passes out in my arms.

Jace is by my side in a second as are the EMTs from the other ambulance. We all watch helplessly as she's loaded in. On impulse, I wrench away from Jace and tell the driver, "I'm her sister."

"Get in, then." He motions and I take the seat next to her and grab her hand. I look up to see Jace's look of disbelief as the doors latch behind us.

We speed away. I smooth the hair from Zoey's eyes and kiss her forehead. Sometimes you've just got to be there for the person who needs you most.

Right now that's Zoey.

Jace will understand when things settle down.

I know it.

Chapter Eighteen

The Same Day

UNFUCKING BELIEVABLE.

I cannot believe that Alex just left like that. She's fucking pregnant. She's high risk. Nothing is more important than our baby, and she's being so careless. I'm so fucking mad but have a little bit of self-awareness to know that I can't talk to her until I cool down. There's no need for me to add to the stress of the situation.

Ronni grabs my wrist. "We should go inside. I'm sure we're being filmed. At the very least, we can try and do some damage control until we can figure all of this out."

She's right. I follow her and Connor back inside The Mission. An officer approaches and asks if we'd all be willing to make a statement. After I confirm that they will not publish anything that's said publicly, I nod to Connor.

"Ladies and gents," Connor's voice booms. "None of us have words to describe what just happened. All of you are valued members of the LTZ and Mission community. We ask that you cooperate with the police and remember you're all under NDA. No one may talk to the press or post on social media without running it past our management. For those who are here with the Rainier Foundation, the same thing applies."

I know that this is going to get leaked no matter what we do. As fucking usual, it's up to me to do some damage control for Ty's bullshit.

The three of us go back into the fated dressing room for some privacy to come up with a game plan.

"I think it's best if I go to Fee." Ronni kisses Connor. "After all her hard work, the night is ruined. Everything she planned is ruined. Someone needs to be there for her."

"I wish Alex had thought of that instead of chasing after Zoey," I grumble after she disappears through a skinny door I hadn't noticed before.

Connor shakes his finger at me. "Ack. No, Jace. Alex and Zoey have been friends since they were wee lasses. She did the right thing to be by her side. Don't make this situation worse by taking it out on her."

"Aren't you furious?" I throw my hands up.

He peers down at me. "Aye, I'm furious at what happened to the band and the night in general. But we don't have any further insight, do we?"

"I have an idea." I shake my head. "More of the same. Maybe this is all for the best. I don't want to do this anymore."

Connor turns over a couple of the chairs so we can sit. "Jace, my brother. You've lived a privileged life. As have I. There's a lot about Tyson's past that I relate to, though. We both had to grow up too soon and support our families because of addiction. It fucks with you. I'm not excusing him, but Ty's a gentle soul. I've never seen him like that. Ever. Let's at least try to remain neutral until we know more. All of us need to stick together."

"With all due respect, you heard him. LTZ is through. He killed our band, Connor." I punch my fist into my hand.

"Aye. So it seems." He stands. "But before all of this happened, he looked happy. Genuinely happy. So, I'm going to reserve judgement. I'll get the crew to start loading up the gear. I'm sure we can get Ty's foundation kids to clean up a bit. I just want to take some of the burden off Zane and Fiona. They're going to have a lot to deal with."

I take a deep breath and look at the man who's been like a brother to me since I was a teenager and he was dating my sister. "You're a stand-up man, Connor. A caring man. I'll do my part too, I'll call Katherine. She's still officially our manager. I'll even sort out social media. Draft a press statement. All the usual damage control."

"Right. Let's reconvene in a bit." He salutes me before heading back into the main room.

Surveying the mess in the dressing room, I decide to ignore it for now. I'm fully immersed in my tasks when a text from Alex comes through.

Zoey's resting. The baby's fine.
I'm taking an Uber back as soon as
her folks get here. Lena's staying
overnight with Mom.

Okay. Sorry for being an asshole.
I know why you left. I was just
worried about our own baby.

I know. I'm fine, though.

Stress is not good for you, Poppy.

Obviously. But I knew I'd be
stressed if I didn't go with her.
Can you trust me to take care of
this baby? Please?

It's not about trust. I'm just
pissed that we're in this situation. Again.

Okay. I get it. What is going on
there?

Fee's devastated. Ronni's with her. I don't know anything else. The police are wrapping up here. Connor's overseeing getting the gear loaded up and the showroom cleaned up.

I'm going to see if I can find Zane before I come back and find out how Carter's doing.

That would be awesome.

I love you, drummer boy.

I love you too, doesn't look like drumming is in my future though.

Be there soon.

I finish with my task list, satisfied that I've done all I can do. I go to find Connor. Everything is packed and put away. Most everyone has left except our crew.

"Ronni says Fiona hasn't heard from Zane. The staff is cleaning everything up. Are you hungry? There's a shit-ton of food that's going to spoil if it's not eaten." Connor motions to the crew. "I say, let's bring them over. Try to salvage their evening at the very least. When will they get a meal like this otherwise?"

It's the best idea, considering. Connor and I lock the doors and bring Pokey, Rex, Angus, and Kimora, The Mission's sound tech, through the dressing room door into Gus. We weave our way through the dish pit to the dining room where Fee, Ronni, and her restaurant staff are plating the food.

"I'm glad this won't be completely wasted." Fee's face is stoic as she hands me a plate.

The food looks stunning. "I'm so sorry, Fee."

She bites her lip. Clearly holding back tears. Her phone rings and buzzes, nearly launching itself off the table. She grabs it just in time. "Zaney, talk to me." She moves briskly to the kitchen for privacy.

Ronni hands a plate to Connor and takes one for herself. "We need to eat this food. She worked her ass off for this and now it's ruined."

The three of us eat. Not because we are hungry. We do it for Fiona, who put her heart and soul into this night. I'm halfway through my meal when Alex texts me.

Alex: "Can you let me in? I'm out front."

When I find her just outside the door, I cuddle my fiancée tight. "God, Poppy. What the fuck?"

"I know." She grabs my hand. "I have some news."

The four of us huddle together. Alex whispers, "Carter is in ICU. He's beat up pretty badly. He had a heart attack. Zane wouldn't tell me anything else until he talked to Fiona."

"She's a mess, understandably." Ronni hands Alex some food. "We're eating what she made for us in solidarity."

By the time we finish, Fiona still hasn't returned. Her kitchen staff takes it upon themselves to clean everything up. Pokey offers to take the band's gear back to the secure storage space. Connor lets the rest of the crew go.

"The police are gone. I think we should go straighten up the dressing room." Ronni looks pointedly at Alex. "You boys take a rest; it's been a long day. Get a drink, there's some phenomenal shit in the bar."

Our girls leave us. I check the time on my phone. Fuck. If the evening had gone as planned, we'd just be taking the stage now.

"Are you calmer?" Connor pours us each a shot of Midleton, his favorite Irish Whiskey.

"Yeah. I texted Mike Pearson, he's working on getting Ty out of jail. Apparently, Carter and Zane aren't pressing charges."

"Good. Good." He swirls the liquid in his glass and takes a sip.

We move to the waiting area at the front of the restaurant and sit in the oversized couches. Neither of us say anything. I mean, what is there to say at this point.

"Alex is pregnant," I say quietly and look up at him.

He nods.

"She's been having serious health issues."

"We all have things we're dealing with outside the band, my man." He takes another sip. "That's life, isn't it?"

I lean back and shut my eyes. "I was looking forward to playing tonight."

"We all were."

"Don't move back to LA." I point at him with my glass, opening one eye to see what his reaction is.

He's about to speak when Alex runs toward us holding up a piece of paper. Ronni is hot on her heels. She skids to a stop and thrusts the paper at me. "Holy hell you guys, we're not supposed to know this, but Carter is Ty's father. This is an official DNA test."

We all look at each other, astounded.

"We've got to assume this is going to get leaked. Jace, you should call Katherine back." Connor nods at me.

I hold up my hand. "No, we aren't supposed to know about this. It's their private business. In fact, none of us should say anything. We can't embarrass Carter, Zane, Ty, and Zoey like that. With all of that said, what the actual fuck?"

Alex takes the paper from me and folds it up, tucking it back in the envelope. "Ronni and Jace, I know you are better at all of this celebrity damage control stuff than I am. I should be the one to bring this to Zoey. She deserves to know about this before anything else happens. I'm going to head back to the hospital and give this to her before she's released. It's what any best friend would do."

"Okay, Poppy." I stroke her hair. "I'll drive you. We've done all we can do for now. At some point, the chips are going to fall where they fall."

Connor grabs our empty glasses and stands. "Aye. Agreed. As for us, we should get the kids."

"Actually, no we shouldn't, Connor. I talked to your mom. She's keeping the twins tonight. We need to stay here with Fee until she's ready for whatever the next step is." Ronni loops her arms through his elbow.

I follow Alex out the door. We drive toward the hospital. I reach over and place my hand on her thigh. "Tell me the truth. How are you feeling?"

She shakes her head. "I'm numb, honestly. Today's been a lot, but this revelation is shocking. Just shocking."

"Doesn't excuse how Ty reacted."

She cocks her head. "Maybe not, but you and I are not an island, Jace. We've been living in a bubble for a while. I love our bubble, don't get me wrong. But...everyone in the band and their significant others are our dear friends. They're our family. I can't—and won't—give up on Zoey. Ever. No matter what. If she's decided that Ty is worth all of this, then I'm not giving up on him either. Neither should you. Be mad. Call him out when the time is right. Don't give up on him."

"What if there's too much water under the bridge, Poppy?" My voice hitches.

She covers my hand with hers. "Then we'll all grab lifeboats and figure it out."

Chapter Nineteen

The Same Day

I TAKE A HUGE gulp of air.

I'm standing outside Zoey's room. I'm terrified of giving Zoey the envelope. As horrific as the day has been for everyone in the LTZ family, she's the one who is married to the man who had a breakdown over paternity results.

I have absolutely no idea if she knew about Carter being Ty's biological father. My guess is no. From what I've pieced together, Ty opened the results when he brought Zane and Carter into the dressing room after sound check. I don't think anyone knew or was prepared for...

Gawd, I wish we could all wake up again and have a do-over of today. I'd give anything to go back in time.

I have to get it over with. Jace is waiting for me in the parking garage. His patience with the entire day is already hanging by a thread, I don't want to push it further than I have already. Truth be told, all I want to do is curl up with him and Lena and be thankful that my family is intact.

And, God willing, growing.

I place my hand on my belly. Take another deep breath. Then move to the doorway. Mike and Olivia flank Zoey's bed. I put on a cheery smile. "Hey, can I come in? The nurse told me you're awake."

Zoey's face lights up. She waves me in.

"They're releasing her tonight. We're just waiting for the all-clear." Olivia gives me a hug. "Mike has one of his friends working on getting Ty out. We still don't have a great picture of what happened."

I keep my mouth shut. I'm going to tell Zoey what I know when we're alone and leave it up to her what she shares with her parents. After they leave, I sit on the side of the bed and grab her hand. Tears seep out of my eyes until I'm fully crying. She's crying too. We weep as only best friends do until she finally speaks. Her voice glitches with each word. "No one will tell us anything. I don't know what's going on, Alex. Your phone went dead and the next thing I saw was Ty getting arrested. What did he do?"

"I didn't see it. According to Jace, after they did their sound check, Ty asked Carter and Zane to meet in the dressing room to discuss something. They were in there a long time before the commotion. Everyone heard Ty yelling. Apparently, he exploded and beat the ever-loving shit out of Carter to the point of unconsciousness. Then Zane beat the shit out of Ty to get him off Carter. Jace and Connor kicked the door down and pulled Zane off Ty. Zane screamed horrible stuff at Ty on his way out the door. Ty said incredibly hurtful stuff to Jace and Connor." I can't help but wince. "He quit the band and told them to fuck off. Luckily, no one was there so it hasn't hit the news. But it will, Z. You need to be prepared."

Zoey shakes her head. Her shoulders slump. "None of that matters, Alex. The only thing that's important to me is Ty's well-being. He was so happy this morning. So excited to play. Something must have happened to set him off."

That's when it's clear to me she doesn't know about Carter. Fuck. I'm going to be the one who tells her. I squeeze my eyes shut and swallow the lump in my throat. I don't want to hurt Zoey. It's the last thing on earth I want.

"Tell me." Zoey squeezes my hand. "Even if it's hard. I need to know."

I unzip my bag and grab the envelope. Squeeze my eyes shut and take a deep breath. Then rip the bandage off when I pull it out and hand it to her. "I'm pretty sure this has something to do with it. When the police were talking to the guys, Ronni and I tried to clean up the dressing room to help Fee out. It was dee-stroyed. As you can imagine, Fiona is devastated. On so many levels. Anyway, I found this. I read it, Z."

Zoey tilts her head. I've never seen her so vulnerable. Ever. I debate whether to tell her the entire truth, because what I've just given her is a lot. If she thinks everyone her husband loves knows his business, I'm sure it will severely damage our friendship. I make a decision. In the moment. I'm going through with a white lie.

Later, I'll beg for forgiveness. I continue, "But, I haven't showed it to anyone, including Jace. And I won't. It's none of our business, but I knew I had to keep it safe. Here."

I hand her the paper.

"What is it?" Zoey takes the envelope. I see a million questions fly through her head when she takes the paper out and reads it. She gasps, her eyes wide. She flutters her hand in front of her face. "Oh. My. God. Help me up, Alex."

I jump up and grab her hands, it's an awkward to say the least. She squints at me and demands, "What is going on right now? Please tell me the truth."

"Connor and Jace are incredibly pissed. Fiona too. I haven't talked to Zane, although I tried when I came with you to the hospital earlier. I'm not going to lie, this might have been the last straw. Ty was completely belligerent. Out of control. Understandably, I suppose. But Zoey? Whatever all of this is about? Ty can't continue to make the band absorb the brunt of his issues. I know he had a bad childhood. But what he did is not okay. It just isn't. Carter could die. I'm not sure where LTZ goes from here." I lay it all out for her. She needs to know what Ty did. How bad it was.

Her face sets with determination. I realize I might have gone too far. Pushed the boundaries of our sisterhood. Of course, she'll take Ty's side, as she should. If the situation were reversed, I'd take Jace's side. In a fucking heartbeat.

She thrusts her shoulders back and the wall goes up. "You don't know the whole story, Alex. Trust me. Don't say something you can't take back. I promise you, there is more to this than any of you know."

"I love you, Z." I squeeze her hand tightly. Exhale a breath I didn't realize I was holding. Try to figure out a way to backtrack and realize I can't. I might as well put it all out there. Trust that we'll get through it. "It's just... Fuck. You're right. I don't want to ever say anything to you I can't take back. Here's the deal. We all have our own lives. Our own struggles. Our own obstacles to overcome. All of those guys have bent over backward for Ty. For years. They have protected him. They have loved him. They have defended him. Ty lives in his own world and doesn't often see what he has in front of him. All of those guys are gems. Actual gems. Over many years, I saw how Ty behaved firsthand. None of them deserved what he put them through then. They definitely didn't deserve what just happened today."

Zoey's lip curls. Her hazel eyes flash with anger. "Okay. I've heard enough. I'm not going to discuss this with you, Alex. With all due respect, if the guys have a problem with Ty, then the guys need to have that discussion. Not you and me. I love you. You're like my sister. But Ty's my husband. He's my only concern right now because he needs me. If that puts me on the other side of the LTZ fence that seems to have been built? Fine."

She lets go of my hand dismissively and starts rummaging around the room, clearly looking for something. We both look up when a doctor comes through the door.

I decide it's time for me to go and I head for the door. "I love you, Z. I hope this all blows over. I really do. Jace and I are heading to my mom's to pick up Lena. Ronni and Connor just left. Zane and Lianne are in the ICU with Carter. Fiona's back at the restaurant trying to recover from the disaster. Text me when you're in a better place. No matter what happens, you're my best friend. I'm always here for you."

I hover in the doorway for a second, but Zoey doesn't even bother to look up or wave goodbye. My heart breaks a little. I'll be devastated if I lose her.

I have to get out of here.

I have to get to Jace.

As I hurry down the corridor, I wonder if I should've held my tongue. By the time I reach the elevator to the garage, I'm bawling. Again. Fucking hormones.. No, it's like the entirety of this shitty day hits me all at once.

I sit down on a bench to collect myself. To reflect on what just happened with my bestie and what it all means. It occurs to me, over this past year, Zoey's surpassed me in the relationship game. She knows her husband. Believes in him. And she'll stand by Ty no matter what. Why? Because she's all in. And that gives her confidence in the face of adversity. Strength in her convictions.

What they have is unbreakable. I saw it in her eyes.

Whether or not our friendship survives, she's just taught me something profound about commitment. Everything I thought I knew has shifted in an instant. Gawd, it's so clear.

I've been operating from a place of scarcity.

Deep down, I've always been scared of losing Jace. I've worried that I'm not enough. I constantly look for cracks in our relationship to justify why I always keep one foot out the door. To justify my failure to commit to him fully. To avoid talking about our wedding whenever he asks.

Jace, on the other hand, operates from a place of abundance.

He's been by my side through every single thing we've ever endured. Not just these past couple of years. Or even this past very tumultuous year. No. Jace presented his heart to me on a silver platter way back in Barcelona. And he's done it again and again and again.

My man's been all-in for over a decade.

Jace's given me space when I've asked for it. Stepped aside when I told him to. Kept our relationship secret when he wanted to shout it from the rooftops. He's even accepted the fractured parts of me I've doled out sparingly. Even when I know he wants all of me.

He deserves so much better than that.

I have no interest in playing it cool anymore. I'm done holding myself back from the man who loves me more than anything else in the world.

I've been so stupid. And selfish. Jace would never, ever hurt me. There's no one on earth who has my back the way he does.

I love him with every single molecule in my body.

I'm going to love him for the rest of my life.

There's no need to protect myself. He needs to know. Now.

I spring up and jab the down button over and over again with my thumb, willing the elevator to get there quicker. When the doors slide apart, Jace is there. I fall into his arms. "I fucked it up so badly. I've destroyed my friendship with Zoey."

"Not possible, Poppy." We ride down to the garage. He guides me to the passenger seat and buckles me in. "It's been an all-around horrible day. None of us are going to get over what happened anytime soon. I think we need to focus on our own family. Keep each other safe."

He moves to shut the door but I grab his forearm. "You, Lena, and this baby are the most important things in my life. Above everything else. I want us to get married. I'm not just saying it, I mean it. If you want to go to Vegas, let's go to Vegas. We deserve to have our own happy ending. I do not want to wait one minute longer to be your wife."

Jace bends down and presses his forehead to mine. Rubs my nose with his. He cups my face with both hands and kisses me. A scorching, soulful promise of forever.

"Yes," he whispers against my lips.

Chapter Twenty

Six Weeks Later

WEEKS LATER, AND I'M still in disbelief.

The three remaining LTZ band members and our loves are trying to pick up the pieces. Operative word, "trying."

Zane, Fiona, and Mia fucked off somewhere. No one knows where they are, but my guess is in Maui. The house they bought last year is a perfect place to take a breather.

Connor and Ronni went back to LA after everything went down. He claims they're still moving to Seattle, but I don't believe him.

Ty's in rehab somewhere in Arizona. Zoey, apparently, is with him.

As for Alex and me? We're taking it day by day. Currently, we're at her mom's house. We decided to stay overnight here so Andrea can watch Lena when we visit Dr. Madison to get an early ultrasound and other tests. Because of her endometriosis and everything else, Alex's pregnancy is high risk. Both of us have shifted our entire focus to doing whatever needs to be done to bring our baby to term.

"Whatcha thinking about?" She uses her index finger to pull my bottom lip down and releases it so it springs back into place. "You're awfully broody at such an early hour."

I capture her lips with mine. Our tongues swirl together. I grip her face with both hands. Our kisses deepen and take on an almost frenzied pace. Like we're starved for each other. For this connection.

Until we hear the door rattle.

We fly apart. Alex's face is bright pink from my stubble. Her nipples are like bullets through her sheer, white tank. My cock is so hard it tents the bedding. I cup it to try to calm myself.

"Mama?" The door handle jiggles.

Alex looks at me and motions for me to pull the coverlet up before getting up to unlock the door. No need, my boner died the second I heard my daughter's voice. Alex unlocks the door and our little girl peers at us. "Hey, sweet girl, is it time for snuggles?"

Lena shrieks and runs to me. I scoop her up and zerbit her chubby cheeks. She sits back against me, grabs a chunk of my hair and sucks her thumb. Alex climbs back into bed, and we sandwich our girl between us.

It's my favorite time of the day.

The three of us are beginning to doze off when Andrea appears in the doorway. "You need to get going. You're used to Poulsbo traffic, not the hell that is Seattle."

"Shit. You're right." I roll Lena, who's sound asleep, fully onto the mattress. She burrows under the covers. I stroke her hair, stand up and stretch. "I'm excited you're far along enough to see Dr. Madison. She'll probably prescribe bubble wrap and bed rest."

She rolls her eyes at me. "If that's the case, I'll at least have time to lounge around and finish up my certifications. The horses should be ready as therapy animals within the next year."

"Uh, I can think of some naughty stuff to do in bed." I waggle my brows at her.

"Don't get your hopes up, Romeo. If I'm on bedrest the naughty stuff will likely be out too."

I glide over to her, wrap her up in my arms and pepper kisses along her jaw and neck. "Well, we've always been creative. I will always find a way to make you come, Poppy."

She playfully swats me away. We dress in record time and get on the road. Shockingly, traffic is light and we're an hour early for her appointment at the clinic. Even at this early hour, the day's already unusually hot, so we decide to get some iced herbal tea and sit in the air-conditioned building. We find a little out-of-the way cubby and plop down. The press has been insane since the debacle at Gus. I'm the least recognized LTZ member, and even I'm getting hounded in public. I'm keeping my shit as low-key as possible.

Alex stares out the window. She's unusually quiet. Her mood has been very up and down since the Zoey incident in the hospital. She blames herself for their rift, which is ridiculous.

"You seem sad, Poppy." We're sitting cross-legged across from each other on a flat, concrete barrier. "Still nothing from Zoey?"

"No."

It makes my blood boil. Alex rode with her to the fucking hospital on the day her husband freaked the fuck out on all of us. She kept the paternity results—which were crumpled up on the floor for anyone to find—discreet. Alex is always there for Zoey. She's called. She's texted. She's apologized. Groveled. A couple days ago, she even texted her about the pregnancy. Hoping it would jar something loose in her BFF.

To no avail, apparently.

It pisses me off. Even if Zoey is still upset, could she just have the common decency to acknowledge Alex? Congratulate us? She knows about what Alex's been through. Yet she's disappeared just like she did after she broke Ty's heart all those years ago. The woman is not my favorite person in the present moment.

"Don't." She leans back on her hands and looks up at me. Her blonde hair cascades behind her shoulders.

"Don't what?" I cock my head. I can't think of anything that will ever make me want either Ty or Zoey in my life again.

She sits back up. Winces. Then places her hand on her flat stomach. "Don't judge her. Let's not have this fight again. We have no idea what's even happened yet. Everyone's scattered. No one's communicating. I trust that she has stuff going on. I mean, Ty found out one of the only people in the world he trusted was his father. Neither of us has any way to comprehend such a thing."

"Poppy. Please. Don't be upset." I take her hands in mine. "I get all that. I do. I'm just over it. Even if Ty apologizes and wants to get the band back together, I don't think that's what I want anymore."

She smiles and quirks her nose. "You, sir, are delusional. I think you're mad because LTZ might truly be over and you were really excited about the band's next chapter. You can lie to yourself, but I know the real truth."

She's fucking right.

How annoying.

"LTZ is truly over. I'm excited for our next chapter. I'll try not to be so negative." I flatten my palm against her stomach.

She covers my hand with hers. "Me too."

"Do you think we'll ever stop caressing our child?" I wink at her and nod to our hands.

This elicits a smile from my girl. "I hope not. I feel like we're protecting her."

I can't help but smile. I'd love to have another daughter. "Do you think it's a her?"

She coyly shrugs. Leans in for a kiss.

We sit holding hands for a bit until it's time to head upstairs for the appointment. We're waiting for the elevator when Alex gasps and braces herself against the wall. She's heaving. Gasping for air.

"Poppy?" I crouch down and look up at her. Her face is contorted in agony.

A second later, her body jolts like she was tasered. She slams her palm on her hipbone. "Jace, help me."

Without thinking, I scoop her up and into the stairwell. Alex clings to my neck. Her guttural moans scare the ever-loving shit out of me. "Talk to me, baby. Tell me what's happening."

"Oh God. It hurts so bad. I'm scared." She starts to become hysterical. Sobbing. Crying out again when a jolt of pain sears through her body.

I manage to get us up the four flights of stairs to reception and scream as loud as I can, "Dr. Madison. We need Dr. Madison. Now. Something's wrong. Help her!"

We're at a clinic, not a hospital. I don't even know if this is a safe place for Alex. People are starting to stare and point. As much as I hate myself for thinking it, I know we need to be somewhere private. I don't want her medical condition to be part of the public's fascination with all things LTZ. Not now.

Not ever.

A man emerges with a wheelchair. Alex sits and allows him to take her back to the examining room. I follow, grimacing because her wracking sobs fill the corridor.

I'm so scared. So helpless.

Dr. Madison dashes toward us in her white coat. "Jace, Alex. What's going on?"

"We were at the elevator when she had a sharp pain. I had to carry her here." My voice is frantic. "What's happening?"

"I need for the two of you to calm down. Let's not panic. I'm going to run a few tests and then we'll fire up the ultrasound to see what's happening." Dr. Madison motions to the orderlies and we follow them down the hall into a private room. "Alex, on a scale of one to ten, how bad is it?"

She whisper-rasps, "Eleven."

Her word pierces my heart. Absolutely devastates me.

All I can do is stroke her hair. Try to keep her settled while the nurse gives her meds and takes her vitals.

Dr. Madison, meanwhile, is taking some samples. She disappears for about twenty minutes and returns with the ultrasound machine. It's quiet while she adjusts it.

Alex has stopped crying. She just lies there. Almost resolute in doom. I pull my chair closer and cradle her head. Kiss her temple.

All the while my belly fills with acid.

"I reviewed your HCG levels. They're lower than I'd like," Dr. Madison says as she prepares the ultrasound. "Let's see what's going on."

We all stare at the screen as the doctor glides it along Alex's belly. I have no clue what I'm seeing. The look on Dr. Madison's face is impassive, but her eyebrow quirks not once, but twice. I catch Alex's eye, The look that passes between us breaks my heart. We know.

We don't want to know.

But we do.

Dr. Madison finishes the exam and turns to Alex and takes her hand. "I'm sorry to say that I'm not able to find any sign of an embryo in your uterus. The ultrasound shows fluid pooling in your abdomen, which indicates your pregnancy is ectopic and has ruptured. We will need to take you in immediately for surgery."

"Now?" I blurt out.

She nods. "An ambulance is on the way to transport Alex to Swedish Hospital up the street. I hope that laparoscopic surgery will be possible, but considering what seems to be a significant amount of internal bleeding, we most likely will have to do an invasive procedure called a laparotomy."

As she explains the procedure and all of the risks my focus is on Alex.

She's staring at the wall like a zombie.

"I'll leave you two alone to discuss, but things are going to move quickly. I'll be back with the paperwork."

"Give me my phone." Alex snaps to attention once the doctor leaves and reaches for it, wiggling her fingers. "Now, will you go outside for a minute and see what we can do about the press? The hospital might give us a private area if they're not overbooked. I just don't want either of us to have to deal with the loss of our baby in public."

At this point, I'll do anything for her. "Okay."

"Jace?" I hear Alex call as I step out of the room. I peer back in at her. "Come back as fast as possible. I'm scared. Really, really scared."

I can't help it. Tears well up. "I'll be back in a second, Poppy. I love you. We'll get through this."

Even I know what the doctor didn't say out loud.

We may not get through this.

And I'll never be able to go on without her.

Chapter Twenty-One

The Same Day

I SHOULD HAVE TOLD him about the cramps.

Last night, after Jace and I went to bed, I felt a sharp pain in my lower abdomen. Kinda like my menstruation cramps used to feel, just twenty times off-the-charts severe. It only lasted a couple of seconds. I didn't bother to wake him up because it was one and done.

After the incident, it was hard for me to relax. I was panicked. One minute I would go from being hot and sweaty and feeling like I was going to vomit. The next minute, I was freezing cold and shivering. Eventually I fell asleep. When we woke up, everything seemed back to normal. No pain. No cramps. No nausea. No weird feverish symptoms.

We had a great morning with our daughter.

Then, on the drive to the clinic, I felt a slight discomfort in my lower abs which seemed to disappear as fast as it came on. I visited the ladies' room while Jace bought us iced tea. I was relieved to find out I wasn't bleeding. There was no discharge. But, a dull pain permeated my entire pelvic area, making it hard to walk. It passed a couple minutes later, and I managed to pull myself together. Even if it took every ounce of stamina I had.

I didn't want to worry Jace. Not when we were mere moments away from my doctor appointment.

I figured we had plenty of time.

Except the little flutters of pain flared and intensified on our walk to Dr. Madison's office. By the time we got to the elevator, I could hardly breathe. A slicing, stabbing sensation in my vagina caused me to crumble. The utter and total agony took it all out of me. If Jace hadn't been there, I would have passed out. No question.

By the time we arrived at the clinic, time began to stand still. Like I was floating. Almost like an out-of-body experience. Maybe it was my coping mechanism.

Because I knew it was all over.

There was no baby.

Our baby was gone.

I'm in the ambulance. We're heading to the hospital where I'm going back in for surgery. After Dr. Madison explained that my fallopian tube likely ruptured, I've been mentally in and out of paying attention. The grief I feel is too deep. Too overwhelming.

The moment we arrive at the hospital, everything happens at lightning speed. The energy is frenetic. I'm being rushed somewhere. Voices above me are either loud and shouting or hushed. They're talking about me like I'm not even here.

Maybe I'm not here. It sure feels like I'm floating away.

My head feels like it's stuck in mud. My body's numb. I know Jace holds my hand. He's whispering to me. Telling me how much he loves me. I can't exactly comprehend what else he's saying. I'm confused. Am I going back into surgery?

The one thing I do know, is if I make it out of this, I'll be irreparably damaged. Losing half of my reproductive system earlier this year felt like I was paying for a crime I hadn't committed. Before that first surgery, Dr. Madison looked me straight in the eye and said, "You will have babies."

I believed her.

And now, it's all over.

I've lost our child.

"Her fallopian tube has ruptured, which means it's too late for a methotrexate shot." I vaguely hear Dr. Madison speaking to Jace as a couple of orderlies run me down the hospital corridor. "I'm scrubbing in now; we are out of time. The blood pooling in her abdominal area will kill her if we don't get her in as soon as humanly possible."

Running alongside me, Jace grips my hand tightly, pleading, "Do whatever it takes to save her. Please don't let anything happen to her."

"Jace," I try to speak.

He doesn't hear me.

"Jace," I croak a little louder.

Everything comes to a stop just before we reach two big double doors.

"Mr. Deveraux, Dr. McLoughlin will show you to where you can wait," someone I can't see says.

"Jace?" I try to squeeze his hand but I have no strength.

He leans over to kiss me. His hair curtains my face. His hands stroke my head. His face is soaked with tears. "I'll be here waiting for you. You're going to be okay. I love you."

"I love you." My lips are moving but I'm not sure if anything comes out. He's so beautiful in his grief. His hair is so long. His jaw is set. Two days' worth of stubble. His teary, green eyes bore into my soul. He holds up one hand like he's waving goodbye before the doors close behind me and he's gone.

Goodbye, my love.

My vision is so blurry. It feels like black fog is forming around my eyes. I can't feel anything. I can hear words but have no ability to make out what's being said or who's saying it. I just want to sleep. Disappear. Get away from this heartbreak.

I'm jolted alert when my body begins to shake uncontrollably. All around me are loud voices and frenzied movement. There's an incessant beeping sound. I can't seem to make out what's happening. I can't gain control over my body. It's just me, Alex, helplessly flopping around on this gurney.

Above me a bunch of masked faces look down. A poke in my arm and my body quiets. Relaxes.

No matter how positive and hopeful you try to be, when life keeps smacking you down, eventually you break. Breaking can be one quick snap, like a twig in a dry forest. Or, hundreds of little minuscule fissures that eventually weaken you to the point where everything just falls apart.

I'm not sure which of these happened. My brain is so foggy, it's hard to analyze.

Maybe it doesn't matter because the end result is the same.

I'm not coming out of this.

I can't believe it's going to end this way.

Chapter Twenty-Two

Two Days Later

IT FEELS LIKE YEARS since I carried Alex into the clinic.

Months since the ambulance ride over to this hospital.

Nearly four hours since Alex came out of surgery.

Twenty-seven hours. That's how long we've been here.

Alex is still in ICU. My family is here. Her family is here. Carter and Lianne are here. Zane and Fiona are coming home from Hawaii to be with us. Connor and Ronni will be here in a couple of days. I texted both Ty and Zoey and haven't heard a thing.

Which figures. If it's not about them...

Fuck. I can't think like that. When Ty was in the hospital with Zoey after her accident, Zane was the only one who stuck around to help him. It's all a matter of perspective, I suppose. If Ty felt half as scared and helpless as I do now, I should be ashamed of myself for not being there. I'll try to do what Alex encouraged before this nightmare began. Reserve judgment.

"Jace." Dr. Madison raises her hand when she sees me. Her hair is knotted and wild. Her eyes are sunken. By the way she trudges toward me, it's apparent she's utterly and thoroughly exhausted. "First of all, I'm so very sorry for the loss of your child."

I bite my lip and breathe out through my nose. "Thank you."

"I want to fill you in on what happened in there. Alex is in for a bit of a recovery. Not just physically, but mentally."

"She's alive. That's the most important thing."

"I need you to understand how lucky we are. If the two of you had been here half an hour later, we would be having a very different conversation. It was clear when you arrived, Alex was going into shock. That's why we called the ambulance the moment we realized how serious her condition was. We made it to the hospital within fifteen minutes. Had her in pre-op minutes later. When we wheeled her into the operating room, Alex had a seizure before we were able to administer the pre-op medications. This accelerated the process. It was clear, due to the complications, we had to perform a laparotomy—a dramatically invasive version of the procedure we did a couple of months ago. We made two large incisions, one across her abdomen and the second for a drain. The damage, it was catastrophic. Her fallopian tube had burst and we couldn't save it. By this point, Alex lost half of her blood. We nearly lost her a couple of times. She's a fighter. She's also very lucky to be alive."

Jesus.

I have no words. I mean, what do you say to that? I just look at Dr. Madison in disbelief.

"She's stable now. We'll want to keep her in ICU until her levels normalize. When we clear that hurdle, you should plan on her spending a bit of time here." She lets out a huge sigh. "I'm so sorry, Jace. I truly didn't foresee your journey ending like this, but sometimes there's no way to predict."

I shut my eyes to block out a wave of pain. When I manage to look at her again, she's regarding me empathetically. "I'm just grateful you saved her life. Nothing matters to me without her."

"If you'd like me to talk to your families, let me know. I'm happy to answer any questions." She reaches over and touches my elbow.

I glance down the hall. Everyone who's made it here is waiting for some news. "No. You've had a rough day too. Can I go in and see her?"

"Dr. McLoughlin has offered to bring you in. Please know that visiting in ICU can be...jarring." She leans forward on her elbows. "She's connected to a number of machines and drips. The fluids we're giving her to keep her hydrated make her look bloated. Her body's been through a huge trauma. She won't be responsive because she's on some very strong pain-killing drugs and sedatives to keep her calm and help the healing process."

Seamus appears behind Dr. Madison. His eyes are rimmed with dark circles and he looks like he could fall over at any moment, but goddamn if I don't want to kiss him for staying. I can't do this alone.

"Jace, I'll be back to check on Alex in the morning. She's in excellent hands." Dr. Madison gets up, touches my shoulder, and leaves.

"Will you bring me to her?" I bury my face in my hands. "I'm losing my mind, Seamus."

He moves over to me and gives me a hug. I cling to him like he's the last person on earth. I need this contact. Anything for a bit of comfort. "Jace." He pats my back. "I'll take you to her, but you have a roomful of people out there who love Alex. Let's give them an update. Then, you'll be free to sit with Alex as long as you want."

I follow Connor's brother to the waiting room where I spent the entire day. The first two people I see are Andrea and Alan, who sit together crying, clasping hands. Alex told me how acrimonious their divorce was, so this is a sight I thought I'd never see. My mom jumps out of her seat when she sees me, crushing me in her embrace. Pops follows. The two of them envelop me. Jordan and Jen stand behind them, their faces solemn. Carter and Lianne sit off to the side, almost hesitant to interfere.

I pull away from my folks. "You have no idea how much I—we—appreciate you all being here. Alex had a rough time, I wanted to come out to see you before they take me to her. Seamus is going to explain what happened. I don't think I can—" My voice breaks in a sob. I try to recover, but it's no use.

My pops wraps his arm around my shoulder. "Jace, go be with Alex. That's where you belong. We're all here for you."

"Okay." I start to go back down the corridor, but I turn back and address Alex's parents. "I'll be with her for a bit, but I know you'll want to be in there too. Just give me..."

Alan holds up his hand. "Go to her."

I nod. Seamus waves an orderly over, who leads me down the hall. A nurse waits at Alex's door. "Mr. Deveraux, before you go in, I want you to know that when you see her like this it's natural to feel helpless and anxious. You and Alex's family should be prepared for hours, even days to go by with no change to her condition. For now, the best thing you can do is take turns sitting by her side. She'll know you're here. Having her loved ones around her will give her comfort and the ability to heal."

Nothing prepares me for seeing my Poppy so weak. I'm absolutely devastated. I can't help but feel guilty for being so greedy. Lena is perfect. She's enough. We were so foolish to play with Alex's health like this.

I pour my heart out to her for hours and hours. Recount our adventures. Reminisce about various places in the world we traveled to. Gush about Lena. The horses. Mitch. Tell her how mad I am we're not married. Confess that I've been stupid and weak for not recognizing she was hurting. Mostly, I just kiss her. Hold her hand. Stroke her hair. Whisper how much I love her and can't lose her.

Beg her to come back to me. To us.

Throughout, various hospital personnel are in and out of her room. Checking her vitals. Changing the bags. Scribbling stuff on clipboards. I even don't notice Seamus behind me. He puts his hand on my shoulder. "One thing I've learned since my surgical rotation is if you don't take care of yourself, you can't take care of your loved ones. Lena needs her daddy, Jace. Alex's mom and dad are here to sit with her. Let them. The thing is, we hope to bring her out of this sometime tomorrow if her vitals continue to improve. My recommendation is you talk to your family. Set up a visitation schedule so you can be with your daughter and keep some normalcy in her life. Hopefully catch some sleep so you're on your A-game when Alex is awake and alert. That's when she's going to depend on you the most."

An hour later, I'm back in Alex's childhood bedroom. My daughter is cuddled next to me. She's sound asleep, her arm flung across my chest. Her little hand clutches a lock of my hair. I turn my face to breathe in her sweet smell. Vanilla cookies. Lena's plump lips puff out little bursts of air.

Silent tears stream down my face. I've never cried so much in one day. The grief is so overwhelming it bears down on me like I'm being compressed by a vise. At some point, I fall into a deep, dreamless sleep.

I'm startled awake by a rapid pinging. Lena's rolled over and is sprawled out on the far side of the bed. More pinging. Discombobulated, I search for my phone and manage to locate it under my pillow, still attached to the charger. I scroll through various texts from the hospital.

Alex's condition is improving. Her mom's with her now. Jen is upstairs with Becca. Jordan and my folks will be back in the afternoon. Zane and Fee are en route. Then a name I didn't expect flashes on my screen.

Zoey:

> Jace, I'm with Ty in Arizona. I only have access to my phone when I'm not with him at the clinic, so I just heard. Is she okay? Please talk to me. I'm overwhelmed with panic. Are you okay? Is she okay? Tell me, what can I do?

Argh. I've got to answer. I hate doing it over text, but I have zero desire to talk to Zoey.

Me:

> She's had a rough time. The doctor's think she'll be fine, but she's going to be in the hospital for a bit. I appreciate you reaching out.

Zoey:

> Jace. C'mon. It's me. Can you talk?

I sigh and shake my head. There's nothing I'd rather not do. I'm exhausted. Drained. Crushed. Yet, she's the one person Alex would want me to talk to.

I'm at Andrea's house with Lena. I can't b/c I'm going back to the hospital in an hour after I give her breakfast. I'll try to find time to call you in the next few days.

Ok. Take care of yourself. Give her a kiss from me. I love you all.

Will do.

"Da Da." I look over at my little girl. She's sitting up in her yellow pajamas adorned with various ducks. My heart melts.

I scoop her up. "Morning. Do you want some breakfast?"

"Where's Mama?"

I stuff down the tears that threaten to spill so I don't upset her. "She's in Seattle. You, me, your aunties, and your nana are going to have an adventure."

"But I want my mama." Her little face quivers. Her eyes fill with tears.

I rock her to me and kiss her forehead. "Your mama loves you, baby. She'll be back soon. Can you be a brave girl?"

Lena grabs my hair and shoves her thumb in her mouth. She nods.

"Okay, let's get some breakfast and we'll record a video for your mom. Won't that be fun?" I get up and carry her downstairs. Jen and Becca are already waiting with a pan of eggs and some pancakes shaped like hearts. "Look what your aunties made."

Becca sits with Lena at the table. Jen leads me into the living room. "How are you holding up? We're happy to stay with Lena all day. Or do you want us to bring her home?"

"Take her back to the house. I want her to have some level of normality. Until Alex gets out, I'll come home for dinner and to sleep. I can just take the earliest ferry out each morning." I make up the new routine on the spot. Mainly, because it's what Alex would want me to do.

Jen throws herself in my arms. "She's going to be okay, little J. I can feel it."

The devastation I felt yesterday has turned into a dull ache. My body feels like it's about a thousand pounds. I take comfort in my sister's arms. It gives me a jolt of strength to get through the day.

On my way to the hospital, I decide that, for now, I'm not calling Zoey back. It's too emotionally draining for me, and everything I have to give must be for Alex now. So, she's just going to have to wait. Zoey always does things on her terms, which is fine, but I've allowed band business and my bandmates' problems to interfere and deprioritize my relationship with Poppy for too long.

Never again.

Getting Alex healthy and taking care of my daughter are the only things that matter.

Everything else will fall into place. Or, it won't.

Either way, once Alex is back to herself again, we can deal with it then.

Chapter Twenty-Three

Two Weeks Later

To say I feel like ass is an understatement.

I'm sure I look even worse. Not that I care. A near-death experience has a funny way of shaking things up.

I'm getting better though; my body feels it every day.

All I know is that I'm alive and I want to live every day to the fullest. Just as soon as I can get myself healed. I take the Tylenol the nurse left for me when I was napping and wonder where everyone is. I'm by myself. I don't remember being alone since I woke up.

At least my brain fog is clearing enough for me to notice these things, so I've got that going for me.

As far as what happened? My memory ends when we were walking to the elevator. I recall having some cramping. There's no way to forget the pain that triggered everything. After that, it's a blank. I woke up and Jace was hunched over my bed, sound asleep. My hand clutched in his.

A week later.

From what Jace and Dr. Madison told me, my fallopian tube essentially exploded. After they stopped the hemorrhaging, it was literally touch and go as to whether I'd survive. They had me in a medically induced coma for almost two days. Then heavy drugs to keep me calm so I could heal.

Heavy, heavy stuff. It seems like it happened to someone else.

It's been eight days since I woke up, and while I'm going stir-crazy, I don't quite feel strong enough to go home. Jace and sometimes a nurse get me up for a short walk up and down the hall three times a day. I'm able to use the bathroom in my room with help, which is so much better than a bedpan, I can't even begin to say.

All in all, considering the alternative, I can't complain. I miss my daughter, though. Terribly.

The door to my room opens. All I see is a ginormous bouquet of orange and yellow flowers that's so big, it barely fits through the doorway. The timing is perfect for some new blooms. Jace made sure the hundreds of bouquets I received were distributed to patients who hadn't received their own. His idea, of course. Sometimes, I can't get over how thoughtful he is under his cool-as-fuck demeanor.

"Who are these from?" I watch as Jace sets them down on the table.

He rips the envelope. Scrunches up his face. "The card says, 'I love you. I want to be there for you. You have to know how sad my heart is that I can't be. I'm so sorry you're going through this. I miss you. Please heal. When you're strong enough, we'll talk—"

"That's really nice of her."

Jace sits next to me on the bed. "It would be nicer if she were here for you."

"You're being way too hard on her." I grab his hand. "She knows I have you. Her husband needs her and she's seven months pregnant. If I'm okay with where things are at, can you please get there too somehow?"

He arches a brow. "Maybe I'm projecting a little."

"A lot. You're the one who told me she texted you and you never called her back after you promised to," I remind him.

He rearranges a few stems before pulling up a chair next to my bed. "Not sorry. Not apologizing. You were my priority. Speaking of which, we're meeting with the grief counselor any minute now. They want you to do a session before you're released."

"You told me. I don't mind getting it over with. I'll do it." I'm truly indifferent. I'm sad, don't get me wrong, but I'm also grateful to even be here. I wasn't a wallower before this happened. I'm not going to start now. "I don't think I need it, though."

Jace doesn't push me. He traces his finger along my wrist. "How's it feel today?"

"Okay. It looks a little better. I adjust my gown to show Jace my scar, which is bright pink and stretches from hip bone to hip bone just under my belly button. "They took the stiches out this morning. I'm actually surprised at what a precise job they did. In a couple years, hopefully I'll be in a bikini again."

He squeezes his eyes shut. "God, every time you show me the scar, I realize how lucky I am you're here."

"Dr. Madison says she's happy with how it's healing and warned me it will look worse for a while before it gets better."

"Speaking of which." My doctor enters the room holding my chart.

"Can you clear me to see Lena?" I beg. "Jace says she's acting out. I just want to get some normality back into our lives."

She thumbs through the pages. "My main concern is your daughter is too young to remember not to jostle you. You're weeks away from healing enough to pick her up. I'd say three to four months away from even considering getting back on a horse. You're starting to look better on the outside, but your insides are still very much in healing mode."

"Is that a medical term?" Jace blinks up at her innocently.

Dr. Madison rolls her eyes. "You rockstars think you're so charming."

We all laugh. Jace has, in fact, charmed his way through this hospital, and everyone knows it. All to ensure that I get privacy. No one wants to disappoint the drummer of LTZ. It's hard to believe nothing about our situation has leaked to the press. I guess they're all still trying to figure out where Ty and Zoey are.

After we go over my four-week physical therapy plan, Dr. Madison looks at Jace. Then at me. "You two have made it through the worst part of the physical side of this. Every day should get better from here. Alex is ready to take some longer walks." She sucks in a breath. "Look, I know you've said you don't need it, but please consider getting some grief therapy. Alex, you've been through an incredible trauma. Now you're leaving here unable to have children naturally. You're a young woman. It may not hit you now, but I assure you there will be triggers. Be prepared." She taps her clipboard with her pen. "We'll be working on hormone therapy, but getting the correct levels may cause your moods to fluctuate. Jace, watching your partner go through this is its own trauma. You nearly suffered a catastrophic and devastating loss. I'm not going to preach— It's up to the both of you to decide what's right for your mental health, but at least I've said my piece."

After she leaves, Jace takes my hand. "Should we schedule something?"

"Look, I'm all for therapy. I didn't start a horse rescue because I'm against it." I dig deep into my soul to figure out what I'm truly feeling. "If I need it someday, I'll be the first in line. I just don't think it's for me. I truly feel if I can at least get home and start grooming the horses, that will be my best way to process all of this and heal."

"I must admit, I'm feeling the same way you do. Everyone is pushing therapy on us, and I'm sure they do that because it's part of their protocol, but I'm honestly just grateful you're here.

I shift a bit in the bed and swing my legs over the edge. "Can we take a walk in the sunshine?"

"That sounds great." He helps me out of bed. "I'm getting you some pasta or something fattening, Poppy. You've lost so much weight."

When I'm upright, I get my bearings and I toe my slippers on. Jace unties my gown and I put a big, loose

T-shirt on. "I know. I'm skeletal. My tits have essentially disappeared."

"Your tits are perfect. I love your tits at whatever size they happen to be at." He smirks.

"Yeah, well, you saying the word 'tits' is mean. I wish we could have sex." I loop my arms around his neck. "I miss feeling you inside me."

He strokes my bony back. "I'd push those thoughts away for a bit, unfortunately."

Hand in hand, we walk through the tiny outside garden. Summer's not quite over, but the smell of fall is beginning to tinge the air. Exhausted, I lead him over to a bench that overlooks Puget Sound. It's so frustrating when I get winded after walking maybe a thousand steps. "Let's sit for a bit."

"Tired?" Jace pulls me back against him. He softly massages the base of my neck.

I can't help but moan. Jace gives me such a sense of peace. My hospital room is chaotic, with nurses coming in and out. Plus, I'm an active girl. Lying around in bed makes me feel atrophied and sore. "Not really. Just getting my stamina back. It feels so amazing to breathe fresh air."

We stay that way for a while. There's something on my mind, and I'm not sure how to bring it up. All I know is, for me, nearly dying has made me realize that life is too short for indulging in insecurities. If I want something, I'm going to ask for it. If I feel something, I'm going to say it.

"You're deep in thought." Jace finishes my shoulder massage and wraps his arms loosely around my shoulders. Enough to make me feel cuddled without disrupting my torso.

I lean my head into his shoulder and look up at him. "I need to tell you something."

"Uhhh?" His face scrunches up because of the most hated six words to ever be strung together.

"No, nothing like that. It's just before all of this...I avoided all things about planning our wedding. After everything that's happened, I wanted to talk to you about it."

He regards me skeptically. "Yeah. Okay. I didn't want to push you. I figured you had your reasons."

"Probably stupid ones, but I feel like it's important to tell you." I'm nervous, but I know that if Jace and I are going to be together, he has to know all of me. Not just the parts I've shown him up until know. Curated parts.

Jace presses his lips together like he's bracing himself.

"My dad cheated on my mom. He had a job where he traveled for work. I was eight, or maybe nine." Every time I think about it, there's a twinge in my heart. "Before it happened, I thought my parents had the perfect marriage. I don't remember them ever being apart. After, it took my mom a long time to get herself back to the woman you know now. It was rough. I was her only confidant. She hated my dad for what he did. I did too, truth be told."

He tightens his arms just slightly. "I'll never, ever cheat on you, Poppy. You're it for me."

"I know you won't." I reach up and stroke the stubble on his chin. "This isn't about you. It's about something that has kept me from allowing myself to be fully there. Aside from this—er, setback, in my mind our life is perfect. You're perfect for me. I was afraid of disrupting our flow."

Jace kisses my temple. "For me getting married to you is making sure our flow never stops."

"It seems stupid to me now, but I've kept waiting for you to decide that island life isn't for you. I truly thought someday you'd say to me, 'Alex, let's buy a house close to Ty and Zane.' Or, LTZ would start touring at the pace you were on before. I mean, even when you mentioned the idea of our own tour bus, I convinced myself that you'd be pissed. Maybe even ditch me if I wouldn't travel with you."

"You realize that all of your inner dialogue was bull-shit, right?" He shakes his head. "My life is with you. When are you getting it through your beautiful, thick skull that I can't think of a better place to raise Lena than on our ranch? And LTZ is through, so..."

I put my finger to his lips. "Don't count on that. You four have something special. And when you work it all out and go back on tour, Lena and I will be with you. My life is with you. Our lives are with you."

"I've never been so scared as when you were in that operating room, Poppy. All I could think about is how selfish I'd been. I'm sorry if I did anything to make you think...uh, believe you needed to give me a baby for us to stay together. It was never how I felt." Jace's face crumples in anguish. "I'd never want you to think my love was conditional."

"Oh, baby. No." I lean up and press my lips to his. It's the first time we've kissed like this in so long. We're ravenous for each other, but Jace holds himself back.

"I don't want to hurt you." He gasps. "I want to fuck you so bad. Now. Just to show you how I'll never, ever leave your side. You're everything, Alexandria LeRoux. Everything I'll ever want or need. Forever."

"Alexandria Deveraux," I say between kisses. "As soon as humanly possible."

"Really?" He cups my face in his big palm.

"Apparently, getting me through a near-death experience was the final test." I boop his nose.

In a strange way, what's happened to me has set me free.

Free to fully open my heart to this amazing man who's loved me for years.

Free to let my walls down.

Free to love him without limits.

Chapter Twenty-Four

One Month Later

I'LL GIVE IT TO Connor, he either goes big or...well, goes bigger.

I thought Zane's house was spectacular, but it's nothing compared to this house. Ronni and Connor bought a mansion on Lake Washington in an exclusive neighborhood called Hunt's Point. Their house is on a secluded little road that meanders to a dead-end. Their place is at the very end of the street on about an acre of full waterfront property. Three-hundred-and-sixty-degree lake view.

"Holy shit." Zane walks backward across the intricate stone driveway. It's a pattern of chevrons in a variety of gray stones. The smooth, modern exterior is magnanimous. Their front door is nearly fifteen feet tall, made out of steel. You'd think it would look industrial, but it's warm and inviting.

I knock on the door, and a woman answers. "Mr. Deveraux, Mr. Rocks please follow me."

They have a butler? Zane and I give each other the google-eye look behind her back and follow her through what looks to be a living room. Flanked by two floor-to-ceiling rolled-steel fireplaces, there are two long, cream couches. Four gray-and-cream-striped chairs, two on each side. The entire backside of the house is a wall of windows. It feels like you could reach out through the glass and touch the deep-blue water.

"Aye. There you are." Connor emerges from the kitchen. And I use the term loosely. It's the size of the entire first story of my house. It's pristine gray and stainless steel with a twelve-burner gas stove and both a ginormous refrigerator and freezer. A mammoth waterfall kitchen island is surrounded by black-leather barstools. The wall of windows with a view of the lake continues into this room as well.

Zane runs his finger along the stove. "I can't show this kitchen to Fee, Connor. I hope you realize we will never visit you or she's going to want to gut our kitchen and start over."

Connor chuckles and motions for us to follow him into an adjacent room, which turns out to be a fully stocked bar on one side and an enclosed glass wine cabinet on the opposite wall. "Obviously, since Ty's not here, the three of us can enjoy a nice, smooth vintage Midleton." He pours out three glasses of Ireland's finest whiskey.

We clink them together and sit in some oversized chairs that are arranged in a half moon toward the window wall. We all take a seat and look out at the water, which laps at the shore just beyond the glass.

"Fuck, Connor. What is this place?" Zane looks around somewhat wildly. He's not one to be outdone in any department, and it would be hard to top this house anywhere in the world.

His big smile overtakes his face. "Ronni loves being by the water. We fell in love with this place. With her Netflix deal? Let's just say it made the decision easier. Plus, the schools are great. It's private and guarded. Lots of kids in the neighborhood for the boys to grow up with. And, it has all the bells and whistles, so it does."

The three of us look back out at the water. As cool as this house is, I'm happy on the island. I love that Lena will grow up working on the ranch and living a normal life. As excited as I am to hang with my bandmates, we have an actual reason for being here. "I suppose we need to get our game plan for tomorrow." I sip the smooth whiskey. It's the most incredible drink I've ever had. "Are we willing to listen to what Ty's going to say? Do you think he wants to get the band back together?"

"Will you stop, Jace." Zane glares at me.

I cock an eyebrow. "Stop what?"

Connor chimes in. "Sayin' the feckin' band's broken up."

"Uh, Ty quit the band. LTZ can't go on without Ty." I sit forward in my seat. "I thought we were discussing the audience Sir Ty requested."

"I'm pretty sure there's more to it than that, my brothers. So, uh. Ehm. Heads up. Ty hasn't been in rehab. He's been in intense counseling." Zane sets his glass down. He looks like he wants to say something else but holds his tongue.

"What?" Connor and I say in unison.

"Carter's been down in Arizona with him. He's in a program for some trauma he's been dealing with since he was a kid." Zane swirls his whiskey in his glass and stares off into the distance. "I've had some sessions with them about the paternity thing."

With all that Alex and I have been through, I've not given much thought about the root of all of this shit. "Fuck, man. I know you've been going through your own shit. How are you coming to terms with it?"

Zane's head tilts to the side. "It's confusing. Carter's all-in and that brings up some old baggage for me. I'm planning on spending time with Ty when he gets back, although Fee is still raw about the entire situation."

We all sit back and look out the window for a bit. Contemplate. Content in our silence. Funny how spending 24/7 with your dudes gives you that sense of comfort, even in silence.

"How's Alex doing?" Connor turns to me. "We've tried to give you some space so she can recover."

I think about it for a second. "She's surprisingly well-adjusted. I'm the one who's a big mess. When the woman you love is hurt, it's literally the worst thing in the world. I hope none of you ever experience it."

"Yeah." Connor nods and looks me in the eye. "Although all our ladies have had a fair share of shit in their lives, the only one of us who has also been through something like that is Ty. When Zoey was nearly killed by that taxi."

"Do you guys have something to say to me?" I look at both of them in succession. "Do you think that I'm the asshole here?"

"I'm going to be honest with you. In retrospect, you got too involved in LTZ's media stuff, Jace, and we were all too stupid to see it. Or put an end to it." Connor points to Zane. "Ty had a lot of baggage. We all knew that. You made it your personal mission to fix things when he acted out..."

I try to interrupt, "Connor, if I hadn't—"

"I know. Look, I buried my head in the sand. It's no secret I was annoyed with him for many years." He holds his hand up so I'll let him finish. "When Ronni was fake dating him, she got to know him on a pretty deep level.

She always suspected he'd been traumatized somehow because she'd also been through it and was convinced she saw similarities. Ty is part of this band. It doesn't take a rocket scientist to know that he was triggered that day. We're older and wiser now. It's time for some changes that all of us need to make. We also need to remember, above all else, the four of us are brothers."

Zane chimes in and gestures to me, "Jace, you always jumped in and just handled shit for us. And we let you. You never took time for yourself. Never prioritized your relationship with Alex. Take it from me, I feel bad that you felt you had to hide it from Ty. It's fucked up that you put her on a backburner for so long. There's not a doubt in my mind that's where your resentment comes from."

"Uh, isn't this about Ty?" I'm shocked that I'm suddenly in the hot seat. And how eerily accurate Zane always is.

"No, it's about all of us." Connor squints and nods.

Zane hops up and goes to the window. "Fee's going to do the reopening in five months. As you guys know, she took a couple of months off and gave her staff some time off too. Everyone is on board and ready for a redo." He turns to us. "I want one for LTZ too. What happened was nuts. It sucked. We were minutes away from making magic happen again."

"I want the band back together too." Connor gets up and joins him.

Both Zane and Connor stare at me. Still sitting with a glass of whiskey that I haven't even yet sampled. "Well, what if Ty doesn't? Isn't all of our fate in his hands? Again?"

"Don't let your past cloud your judgement, Jace." Zane walks over to me. "Remember, you and Ty were close. As far as I can tell, it's only been the past year or so that you've had this attitude about him. What the fuck, man?"

I can't help but sigh because Zane's correct. I'm certainly not ready to admit it to him yet. Not until I see Ty firsthand when we meet at Zane's tomorrow. I don't want to make promises. I also don't want to make excuses. "I'll try to be cool. I just want to know what we're dealing with. I don't have it in me to go through any shit with him again this year. Or ever, truth be told."

Zane puts his hand on my shoulder. "In case it isn't clear, Connor and I wanted to talk to you, Jace. That's why we're here. Connor and I both want LTZ to continue. I'm ninety-nine percent sure Ty wants to continue.

Before we all see him tomorrow, we needed to ask you if you want to continue too. You are just as important to LTZ as Ty is. What do you think? Do you want LTZ to continue?"

"I don't know," I confess. "I've just been come through hell. I find myself wanting to be with Alex every minute of the day. I don't think you guys realize how close I was to losing her. She's still recovering, you know."

"Fair enough." Connor raises his glass. "We all have to be in, or it's not happening. Give it some thought."

It's funny. Coming into this meeting, I was adamantly opposed to having the band continue. Alex was the one who told me to come in with an open mind and an open heart. She could be bitter and angry about all she's lost, but she's not. She's Alex. Positive. Looking for the good. Believing the best.

I owe it to her and to me to take my time. Decide what I want. What I need.

Maybe for the first time, ever.

I'm lucky to have the woman and friends behind me to give me the space to do it.

For that, I'm grateful.

Chapter Twenty-Five

The Same Day

IT'S A BEAUTIFUL FALL day. My favorite time of year.

Our entire property is surrounded by maple trees. They're at the stage I love most. Orange, yellow, and red curtains of fire. For me autumn is the season which symbolizes new beginnings, not spring. The crisp air and the smell of winter coming always makes me feel the most alive.

Especially this year.

The year I'm lucky to be alive.

I'm sitting on the porch swing. Becca and Lena are feeding the horses. Jen is doing my barn chores because I'm still not allowed to do anything strenuous. My body is healing, but not quite healed. There's an upside. Between Jace, my mom, Jen, and Becca, I never have to lift a finger.

With little to do, I take comfort in gazing out across the land that I worked so hard to acquire. There is no place I'd rather live.

"You've got quite the Zen aura going on." Jen emerges from inside the house and sits next to me, wrapping the quilt she brought out around her.

I take a long sip of my coffee. "Just waiting on my dad. Jace is over at Connor's for the LTZ pre-Ty meeting."

"Ah, he's back from rehab tomorrow, right?" Before Becca, Jen hung out with the band a lot when she was younger and still dating Connor. She knows all the guys from back in the day. "He's been gone a long time. Hopefully, it sticks this time."

I've texted with Zoey once or twice after my near-death experience. She's made a lot of effort; I've made some too. Jace hasn't completely come around yet, but she's my best friend. We'll get through this. "Yeah. We're all meeting at Zane's after his flight gets in."

"That seems like too much pressure." Jen squints at me.

I shrug. "Zoey set it up. I guess we'll have to see."

Becca and Lena approach hand in hand. As soon as Lena sees me on the porch she runs toward me at full speed. Bounds up the stairs and skids to a stop just before she plows into me. "Mama, I feeded the horses."

"You're such a great helper." I gather her against me. Becca gives her an assist to sit in my lap. I'm still not supposed to lift over twenty pounds, so I don't ever risk it. "Are we snuggling until your grandpop comes to get you?"

"Yah." Lena is so delicate and careful with me, I can't wait until we are normal again. Until I'm normal again.

Gawd, I know I'm a terrible patient. Not because I'm needy. It's the opposite. I hate being helpless. No, that's not it. I hate needing help. It's the most annoying part about waiting for my body to heal from such a traumatic experience. It's also why I'm obsessed with doing physical therapy. And walking twenty thousand steps per day. I want my old life back. Stat. Hence, my obsession with getting strong.

A car approaches. My dad's Mercedes Maybach GLS crunches the gravel on our driveway. Lena hops off my lap and runs to greet him as he steps out of his ridiculously expensive SUV. "Hey, baby Lena!" He picks her up effortlessly and twirls her around.

"I's not a baby, Grampop" She sticks her lower lip out as far as it will go.

The corners of his eyes crinkle. "I forgot you're already forty years old."

"No I's two." She holds up three fingers, and I stifle a giggle.

My dad listens to Lena tell him about feeding the horses for a bit while Becca, Jen, and I hold our giggles at how darn cute she is. My daughter is so very serious when it comes to the horses, and I do not want her to think I'm laughing at her. Or to do anything that discourages her in any way.

"I'll go get her bag." Jen pops up and disappears in the house.

I touch her arm. "Can you and Becca take Lena and feed her a snack? I'd like to chat with my dad for a bit."

"Of course." The three of them go into the house.

My dad smiles at me. His silver hair gleams in the sun. Even on the weekend, he's dressed up. Dark jeans. Crisp, gray shirt. Loafers. I sprint down the steps and give him a big hug. "You look handsome."

"My beautiful daughter." He clings to me like I'm drowning. It's ironic. For a man who's never been overly demonstrative, ever since I almost lost my life, he's amped up the affection by ten thousand.

"Walk with me." I pull away and walk backward toward the barn.

He looks down at his shoes, then the dusty ground, then at me. "Uh?"

"Forget your shoes. I want to show you something." I hold my hand out and wiggle my fingers. He takes the hint and I lead him to where Gloria and Samantha are poking their noses out.

We step inside the barn and I pat a bale of hay. Reluctantly he sits, balancing himself at the very edge. I sit cross-legged next to him.

He startles when a horse whinnies. "Jesus, I'm not sure where you got the stinky animal gene, Alexandria, but the smell in here is something."

"I'm going to marry Jace." I ignore his comment. He's always joking with me. Or joking at my expense, more like it. I've done so much soul searching while recuperating. I'm not one to dwell on things, but I've come to many realizations about why I've avoided committing to Jace. There're a million things I want to get off my chest.

"Of course you are." He gingerly scoots back just a little on the hay. "We could have discussed your wedding over a glass of wine. How much do you need?"

I can't help but look at him slack-jawed. "Dad, we don't need your money."

"Ah, is he going to ask me for my blessing? How much can I mess with him?" He grins from ear to ear.

I fold my arms across my chest. Think better of it and pull up the hem of my T-shirt. "Did you see my scar?"

He glances at the dark-red slash under my belly button and looks away. "Jesus, Alex."

"Yeah. Jesus, Alex." I let my shirt drop. "That is the scar that will forever remind me that I will not be able to have children with the man I love. Children I didn't even want until I was able to let myself love him fully. I don't want to make a big thing. I'm not here to chastise you. But I do want to say my piece because it's taken me far too much time and a hell of a lot of pain to get to the place where I feel worthy of Jace's love."

My dad unbuttons the top button on his shirt and shifts on his seat. "Uh, okay. Um, I'm not quite sure where this is going..."

"You left mom. I remember the two of you being so in love. You and I had all these little fun things we did. Like picking huckleberries. Cycling around Greenlake. Sneaking chocolate from the pantry. I thought my life was perfect. I thought I had the perfect family. Then, all of a sudden, you were gone. With that woman you ran off with." I shudder a bit because I've pushed these feelings of resentment down so far it's hard to dredge them back up. "I remember Mom begging you to stay and instead you moved out of state. When you came back to Washington, you were already married to someone else."

"Liz." He nods, almost like he didn't hear everything else I said.

"Yeah. Liz. And each time I'd visit when you still lived in Seattle, you criticized everything I did. Everything I said. It was awful. Do you know, I was psyched when you moved over here to the island? Knowing you'd be so far away gave me the best excuse to stop visiting. I rarely saw you after that. On purpose."

He holds up a hand. "Wait just a second, I always came to—"

"Yeah, you showed up to some of my milestone events, but even then you couldn't wait to get a dig in here. A dig in there. You even told me I was stupid when I decided against college."

He tilts his head to the side. "Uh, it was stupid. I still think that."

"Even after I made millions? Started my own business at eighteen?" I suck in an angry breath. "It didn't even dawn on you to encourage and compliment your daughter instead? I wanted you to say you were proud of me. I moved out here partially so I could get spend more time with you. As an adult. But you don't have any interest. Do you realize this is only the third time you've been on my ranch in the three years I've lived here?"

He takes everything I say in. I can actually watch him process it in his head. Like a little brain computer. Whose output isn't the greatest. "I'm not sure what to say."

"There's no need to say anything." I shrug. "I've come to terms with the fact that you don't value the person I am. You never have."

He reaches for me and I duck away. Physical contact isn't what I want—or need—at the present time. Dad frowns. "Look, I'm sorry if I hurt your feelings. In my defense, I always felt like you were judging me about leaving your mom. Picking at me too."

"You are my dad. And, you're spot-on accurate. I was judging you. I probably still do, especially now that I'm a mother." I challenge him by not breaking eye contact.

"What do you want me to do, Alex? I can't relive my life." He stands. "You can't blame everything bad that's happened to you on me."

"Do you not understand that by essentially abandoning me, I truly believed that Jace could never love me enough to stay?" I stand and face him. Fists clenched at my sides. "I adored you. I worshipped the ground you walked on. Then you were gone. I was so envious of Zoey and her relationship with her dad. I'd hear about how you spent time with Ariel and not me. So, I just buried my feelings. Acted like I didn't care until I actually believed it. Gawd, I became a closed-up version of you until I pulled my head out of my ass."

He shakes his head. "Okay. Okay. Fine. If it makes you feel better—"

"No! None of this makes me feel good. I don't want to hurt you. I've just been through a huge trauma and I have to get this all out on the table if we are going to move forward."

Dad sits back down, almost resigned. "Say whatever you need to, Alex. If it helps you heal or get past whatever it is that you resent me for, I want that too."

"Do you remember that after puberty, I told anyone who would listen that I didn't want kids?"

"Yeah, I always thought it was just a bit of drama."

I clench my teeth. "Uh, no. It was because I was worried. I didn't want any of my future kids to feel as bad as I did when whoever their dad was left. It became my mantra."

"Jesus." My dad buries his face in his palm. "You really felt that bad?"

"A girl's relationship with her dad is important. I needed you, and you always spent time with Ariel. She was your perfect daughter. Never me."

He starts to object, then thinks better of it and gestures at me to continue.

"I'm going to tell you our story. You might not know this, but Jace told me he loved me one summer in Europe. I was twenty-three and we had an epic never-ending adventure. I probably already loved him, but that summer I fell harder." My eyes shut and I can't help but smile remembering our time together.

My dad's lips are pressed together in a thin line. Like he's afraid to speak out. As he should be.

I purse my lips and continue. "The thing is, I was scared. LTZ was his life. How could I fit into it? Except he begged me to be official with him. Be his girlfriend. He wanted us to come clean to the band. Have me tour with him. I flatly rejected the idea outright because of how scared I was to put my career on hold when I believed we'd never make it." I pause to look directly into my father's eyes. Will him to give me some emotion.

He keeps a placid expression on his face and nods for me to continue.

So I do.

"Jace doubled down. He wouldn't take no for an answer. The tour ended and I booked a couple jobs. Jace rented a villa in Italy. It was the best time, but I was freaked out. He kept trying to convince me to go with him. I kept pushing back. As a compromise, I agreed to come home and spend time in Seattle with him. To talk about our future. Meet each other's families when we were both home…"

"You never brought him to meet me." Dad crinkles his nose and looks to the sky.

I roll my eyes. "Uh, no. I didn't. By then, I'd missed my period even though I'd been on the pill for years. I was freaked out. Except somewhere inside me a glimmer of optimism took root. A possibility that he and I could work. We could be together. We could make a family together." I take a deep breath. "So, he had some band thing after the day I spent with you and Liz. Do you remember? You had a lunch at your house for me and all the neighbors."

"Of course. It was a great barbeque. Everyone thought you were wonderful." He folds his arms and juts out his chin.

"It wasn't wonderful for me, Dad." I grimace. "All afternoon you made mean jokes about my travel influencer career. You poked fun at my volunteer work. The entire time I was there, you essentially roasted me. It was mortifying to be humiliated by my own dad in front of his friends. I got the fuck out of there. By the time I drove onto the ferry, I was furious. Wounded. But, also in a panic. All I could think about was how stupid I was. How my life was over because I was knocked up by a dude who was leaving on tour in a month. How embarrassed you'd be. Do you know what I did?"

Dad shakes his head. "No."

"When the pregnancy test was negative, I took my anger at you out on him. I said some very hurtful things to Jace. About how happy I was not to be saddled with a kid whose father wouldn't be there. I took all my frustration from the day and directed it at the man who loved me more than anything in the world. Even after I eviscerated him, he wanted me to stay. When he couldn't convince me, he dropped me off at Mom's. I'll never forget how devastated he looked when he drove off. But also resigned. Like he'd grant me what I asked for. So he did. He let me go." I shrug. "Except, he never wanted to leave me. He did it for me. I'm the one who drove him to it and spent two long years convincing myself I'd made the right decision."

Dad moves toward me tentatively but thinks better of it. Plops back down. "God, Alex. I didn't realize I'd hurt you so badly."

I take a minute to breathe. "You did."

"Are you finished?" He's holding back, trying to be patient. He's not succeeding.

"Almost. I'll finish my story." I wrinkle my nose. I've waited a long time to talk to my dad and get this shit resolved. He's going to listen to me today. "Okay, so Jace and I lost touch for a couple of years. Other than the times I was hanging out with Zoey, I was miserable the entire time we were apart. I felt like I'd lost my soulmate. Then, Jace and I randomly ran into each other at Coachella. It was like we'd never been apart. Except, I still wouldn't throw caution to the wind and agree to be with him publicly. This time, I used Zoey's heartbreak as my excuse."

My dad's entire face is pinched with confusion. "Why?"

"She was still broken up about Ty, I didn't want to rub my relationship in her face. We were together. He even moved out here, but essentially, I hid our relationship and made him do the same."

"Ah. Alex." Dad palms his forehead. "I don't understand what that has to do—"

I'm not interested in my dad's commentary so I plow ahead. "Before we were a couple and we were just friends, he always talked about having kids someday. After my pregnancy scare and reaction, he told me I was his family. Said if I didn't want kids, he would be fine because he wanted to be with me. No matter what." Tears are flowing now. "You know what? I let him make that sacrifice. What's embarrassing is it was only after facing infertility that I realized I'd never given myself the chance to decide what I truly wanted. I didn't give myself the chance to figure out how I truly felt about having kids with Jace. You know why? I didn't want to ever be responsible for giving birth to a child who felt abandoned like I did."

Dad winces. Squeezes his eyes shut.

Silence.

For what feels like days.

I have to fill the void.

"I did know that I wanted Jace." My voice is softer now. "When we adopted Lena, I saw firsthand what an incredible dad he was. And I realized that I'm a decent mom. I love being her mother. The three of us making a family together changed something inside of me. I wanted to give the man I loved a bigger family, because I finally started to trust him to not be you. I almost lost my life trying to give him a baby," I sob. "And now I'll never be able to. And he's still here. Committed. In love with me. Flawed, fucked-up infertile me. He's truly in it for the long haul. How shitty that it took nearly dying for me to trust Jace wholeheartedly."

"You deserve a love like that." My dad finally squeezes me to him. "But I can't erase the past. What can I do to be better in the future?"

"Nothing." I exhale heavily but feel lighter than I have in decades. "Just be yourself. I do love you. I do want you in my life. I don't need anything. I don't want anything. I just want Jace, Lena, and I to have a happy life together and with our extended family."

"I'm sorry." He tilts my chin up with his forefinger. "I really am. If I could grant you one wish, what would it be?"

I smile through watery eyes. "Easy. I want you to be the very best grandfather to Lena. Can you do that?"

"I will try my best, Alexandria." He hugs me.

"That's all I can ask."

Chapter Twenty-Six

The Next Day

I THINK A LOT about the night I almost lost her.

Sure, there was terror. Sorrow. Confusion. Anger, even.

For me, the worst thing was utmost certainty if I lost her, I'd never find what we have again. This is once-in-a-lifetime shit. Sure, I love Alex. She loves me. Our love for each other is a given. Everyone knows, though, that love isn't always enough to sustain for the long term. What Alex and I have transcends love. We are two souls who have found peace in our togetherness.

I've always known it on some level. Trusted it. Even when we were apart, something in me always knew we'd find our way back. We had to. There's no Jace without Alex and no Alex without Jace. We're meant to be together.

As for Alex? Hell, she's known it too, but I'm certain it's taken this near-death experience for her to let herself trust it.

It's beautiful. Despite all that she's—we've—lost, for the first time in our relationship, Alex is peaceful in our love. I wouldn't trade where we're at now for anything.

"I've come to terms with what's happened. Jace and I are still in a bit of shock about how it all went down. It's hard to fathom, I didn't even know what endometriosis was not too long ago. Let alone how it would affect us." Alex runs her fingers through my hair as she talks.

We're at Zane's house, waiting for Ty and Zoey to address us. Connor is staring out the window at the city. Zane is chatting with Carter and Lianne. I'm sitting next to Alex while Fiona and Ronni grill her a bit.

"Well, shit. How could you? It's not like you check any of the risk-factor boxes." Fee blows a huge gust of air out. "I've been scared to get pregnant because of my own risk factors. I nearly died giving birth to Mia. Now I'm thinking I should take it seriously. I'd love for Zane and me to have another child. Maybe even two."

Alex tenses just a little. As well-adjusted as she is, it's still such a blow for her to have gone from being blissfully ignorant about her fertility issues to losing any ability to conceive in such a fleeting period of time.

"God, between the four of us ladies, we sure know how to amp up the LTZ drama." Ronni shakes her head. "Are you so incredibly sad, Alex? My heart hurts so bad for you."

Alex shifts in her seat a bit. "I am sad. It's a weird sad, though. When the pain started, I knew it was the baby. When I woke up in the hospital, it was devastating to hear what happened. I braced myself for an even deeper sense of grief. The strange part is, while I'd never wish this on any of you ladies, the entire experience has filled me with such a deep sense of gratitude. I've never felt as settled. Or at peace. I have more than most people could ever hope for."

"I feel the exact same way, Poppy." I snake my arm around her. Kiss her temple.

"You two are so freakin' adorable." Fiona exaggeratedly swoons.

Ronni leans in, conspiratorially. "Are you nervous seeing Zoey? She's due any day now."

She doesn't get the chance to answer because the doorbell rings.

All the air in the room turns charged. None of us know what to expect. Zane, who is sitting next to his mother, doesn't move so Fee jumps up and dashes to the front door. We can all hear Ty, Zoey, and Carter saying hello in the foyer and then the three of them are standing in the living room. We all stare. Nobody knows what to do or say.

Ty looks as relaxed as I've ever seen him. Zoey, whose belly protrudes two feet in front of her, catches my eye. If she's pissed I never returned her texts or calls, her expression doesn't show it. Even if it did, I'm still not sorry. Her expression softens when she sees Alex. When Alex catches her first glimpse of Zoey, her hand clutches mine in a death grip. I look down and her knuckles are almost white. Her breathing is shallow. Concerned,

I try to catch her eye. She glances at me briefly then shakes her head and returns her focus on Ty, who is now helping Zoey into an oversized armchair.

Carter stands behind Ty and grips his shoulders. "Guys, I appreciate you all coming here today. Ty and I have a few things to say. I sincerely hope that it will be our first step to healing."

Connor, who was at the window when they came in, crosses the room to sit next to Ronni. Fiona takes a seat next to Zane and Lianne. I wrap my arm around Alex's shoulders, bracing for what comes next. I'm not sure why, but I'm nervous.

Zoey whispers in Ty's ear before he nods at her and faces all of us. "I don't know how much all of you know, but it's no secret I've been in Arizona at a clinic that specializes in mental illness." Ty's voice warbles a bit before he clears his throat and embodies his rock-star persona. How he manages to shift into it so effortlessly, still boggles my mind. "Specifically, I was diagnosed with CPTSD a few years ago, and I kept it from everyone. Including Zoey. I thought it would be easier if you all thought I was an addict."

I can't help but look over at Connor. He's as shocked as I am. Alex sucks in a breath beside me and rests her head on my shoulder.

Carter moves around to sit on the arm of Ty's chair. "I've been with Ty at the treatment facility. It turns out that I also have CPTSD, which led to my addiction issues."

Ronni blurts out, "What does CPTSD mean?"

Alex begins to tremble next to me. I try to focus on what Ty's saying as he explains his diagnosis, but she's clearly not doing well and my priority is her. She whispers into my ear, "As soon as he's done talking, can we please go?"

I nod slightly so as to not tip off the room. I want out just as badly.

Ty turns on his superstar power to address us, almost like he's on stage. "I know all of you have some idea of how I grew up. My mom was an addict. But there was a lot I never told anyone. The truth is, from the time I was a young child my mother beat me. Tortured me mentally. Allowed others to abuse me. Because of my CPTSD, I've lived in a constant state of fear. My entire life I've felt like an outsider. I didn't understand how I fit into the world.

Or how to trust those closest to me. I'm proud to say I'm a survivor. But I am living with mental illness. And I always will."

Holy fuck.

Holy ever-loving fuck.

Alex chokes back a sob but then bursts into tears. Fiona and Ronni are bawling too. Zane, Connor, and I try to keep eye contact, while comforting our women. Still, I feel like the walls are closing in. From the expression on my bandmates' faces, none of us had a clue.

The entire energy of the room is charged. Sorrowful. Everyone is whispering to each other.

Zoey claps her hands. "Everyone, please. Let Ty finish. This is important for his healing process. It's a big deal for him to be open and trusting with all of you."

The look that Ty and Zoey exchange is monumental. It reminds me of my mom and dad. Like the two of them have fused into one functioning body. Clearly buoyed by her support and clueless about how shocked all the rest of us are, Ty continues, "My mom died, as you know, right before Zoey and I got married. It wasn't long after I told her about my abuse. Then my diagnosis. By this time, she was pregnant so we started working with my therapist. I was doing really well. Then a lawyer contacted me about my grandparents' estate.

Ty gulps air and blows it out in a whoosh. Wriggles his fingers and shakes them out. "A couple days before the...incident, I found out I'd inherited a shit ton of money. And, access to my paternity results. Never in a million, trillion years would I have thought Carter was my dad. When I opened the envelope and saw his name? I blacked out. All of my trauma caught up to me and I lashed out. For the record, I'm incredibly grateful that the man I've always considered to be my father is actually my bio dad."

Carter beams. "For the record, I was shocked too. I'm not proud that I don't remember sleeping with Tyson's mother. But I've always thought of Ty as my son, so really the only thing that's changed is the fact our blood matches."

My head is like a ping-pong ball today, trying to keep up with all of these truth bombs. Zane stares at Ty and Carter. Fiona's jaw is clenched. Lianne looks like she'd like to be anywhere but here. As shocking as this news was months ago, seeing Ty and Carter united together today makes it all too real.

Ty sucks in a breath and catches my eye before looking at Zane and then Connor. "I'll shut up now, but before I do. I'm sorry. I said horrible things to all of you. Things I truly didn't mean. I can't expect any of you to understand. This information is probably, well... It's a lot. I just need you all to know while I'm never going to be cured, I've done everything in my power to learn how to manage my CPTSD. I understand if you don't want anything to do with me. If the band is truly broken up. I hope that isn't the case, because I was so fucking excited to start things up again. No matter what happens, all of you are my family. I hope you'll find it in your heart to forgive me. To learn more. To talk to me. I'm an open book. I'm not hiding anymore. And I'm not going to let what happened fucking define me anymore."

Ronni, who is still sobbing, kneels next to Ty. Grasps his hands. "I understand, Ty. I'm sorry you felt so alone for so long. You're a good man, sweetheart. You deserve happiness. I'm here for you. Connor too."

Connor doesn't say a word but acknowledges what she says with a slight head tilt.

My arm remains wrapped around Alex, who's crying so hard she's shaking. Seeing Zoey on the verge of giving birth is too much for her today. She's holding it together, but only by the most delicate thread.

Zoey's gaze is fixed on Alex. Her eyes soften when Alex begins to tremble and she moves to get up. I hold up my hand to stop her. I'm not a complete asshole, I'd never keep them apart. It's just not the right time. I'm certain Zoey doesn't know why Alex is having such an emotional reaction. I'm also certain if Zoey hugged Alex right now, my Poppy would have a breakdown in front of the entire group. Not happening on my watch. "Not right now, Zoey. We have our own things going on, and she can't handle this."

"Alex?" Zoey ignores me but remains frozen in place. "What can I do? Please—"

Alex chokes out, "Give me a day or two, Z."

It's time for me to take charge. We're done for the day. I'm taking Alex, picking up Lena and the three of us will go back home into our bubble. "Guys, we've gotta head out. I'm glad you're dealing with your shit, Ty. As Alex said, give us a day or two to process."

When we walk past him and out the door, Ty hands me a piece of paper. I take it, but after I get Alex settled into the front seat, I crumple it up and toss it into the back. Not my priority right now. When I get into the driver's side, I turn to Alex. "Talk to me, Poppy. I know it was hard for you to see Zoey so heavily pregnant. Is that what's wrong?"

She nods. Unable to talk for a minute. When she finds her voice, it's shaky and broken. "I didn't expect it. I'm happy for her. I am. It's just...too much. I want what she has. Well, maybe not all of the Ty drama, oh holy hell—I'm such an asshole."

"Well, then I'm an asshole too." I tip her chin up so her eyes meet mine. "I feel exactly the same way."

Alex places her hand on my thigh. "Can we go somewhere? Just you and me?"

"Now?"

She nods. Tears pool in her eyes. "Mom will keep Lena tonight if we ask. I just need a break—"

My lips crush hers. I know what she needs, and I'm going to give it to her.

Whenever she wants.

However she wants.

Because LTZ be damned, there is no limit to what I'll do to make Alex feel like herself again.

Even if it means turning my back on my band.

Chapter Twenty-Seven

A Little Over Two Months Later

WE ARRIVE AT TY and Zoey's house, which is absolutely gorgeous. The gold and silver holiday decorations are abundant but tasteful, fully on point. The food smells amazing. Something tells me, after three years' running, Christmas Eve is going to be a tradition at the Rainier's Seattle house for many years to come.

All the holiday spirit is cool and all, but today's extra special for me. Jace and I get to see my godson, Oliver. He's nearly two months old and I've only seen him when all the kids came to the ranch for the holiday horse pictures.

Yeah, that's going to be a new LTZ tradition too.

Zoey's been incredibly understanding about my need to process all that happened this past year, though. So has Ty. Even though we essentially ghosted them for a bit, they trusted we had our reasons to go dark after Ty's bombshell announcement.

After all, the two of them have made a career out of dramatic disappearing acts. They can hardly cast judgment.

As for me, gawd, I thought I had it all together. I truly believed I'd come to terms with what happened. Of course, classic me—bury my own feelings and pretend everything is fine.

Oh, how wrong I was. When my best friend walked into the room looking like she could give birth any second, I realized one sad truth. I'd never grieved our baby. All my focus—and Jace's, truth be told—was on healing the severe physical trauma to my body. Mourning the loss of my fertility, maybe.

Never the loss of our baby.

How did I forget such an important piece of the puzzle?

The second Zoey walked into the room and Jace felt my reaction, he knew what was happening. And he was prepared.

Within seconds after we rushed out of Zane's house, Jace triggered the plan he'd made to honor our baby and what happened to us. Yes, to us. Not just me. He wanted to help us find our way forward. To acknowledge and be at peace with our new normal.

That night, he drove us to his folks' house. They were away in Mexico, so we had the entire mansion to ourselves. We bundled up in thick coats, grabbed a couple of heavy blankets and sat at the end of the dock. One by one, we floated six votive candles, perched on beautiful poppy biodegradable paper lanterns, out into Lake Washington. One for each week of our baby's life. We cried for him. Or her. We'll never know. We cried for ourselves. We cried for our baby who never had a chance to live.

Then we snuggled watching the candles float in all directions until the flames flickered out.

Back at the house, he built a roaring fire. Piled soft blankets onto the plush carpet in front of it and we made love until dawn.

The next afternoon, we picked Lena up and flew private to "our" villa in Italy. The place was as beautiful as we remembered. While it was too cold to swim, we blended in with the locals for six glorious weeks. Rested. Hiked. Slept. Tackled sightseeing like the bosses we are. Ate great food.

Most of all, we spent quality time with our daughter.

Oh, and we got married. A tiny ceremony, just for us. We'll have a traditional event for our family, bandmates, and friends in the new year, but I didn't want to wait another second to be Mrs. Deveraux.

Jace waited for me long enough.

We arrived home to Seattle yesterday afternoon, and even though Lena kept us up half the night because of the time change, there was no way we were going to miss tonight. She's got a death grip on my neck. She's exhausted.

Ty greets us warmly. Zoey is nowhere to be found.

"She's not feeling well after the long flight, could I lay her down for a bit?" I'm hoping a nap will help with her cranky clinginess.

"Of course, take her into our room, Zoey's back there with Ollie." Ty gestures to their bedroom.

Excited, but nervous, I make a beeline toward the door. Zoey's placing Oliver in his bassinet and doesn't look the least bit surprised to see me.

"Come see your godson." She reaches her hand out. I go to her and we hold hands and look down at the most beautiful child outside of Lena.

I can't help it, tears well up in my eyes. "He's bigger. And so beautiful."

"Mama. I's sleepy." Lena scrubs her eyes with her fists.

Zoey reaches for her. "Lena do you want to take a nap with your cousin Oliver? You can sleep on the big bed."

Lena buries her face in Zoey's hair and sucks her thumb. Together we tuck her under the blanket. I stroke her hair until her eyes close and she's out.

"I have the baby monitor, let's let them sleep." Zoey and I step into the hallway and shut the door.

I can't help it, I throw my arms around her and we both are sobbing messes. I missed her and briefly confess what happened with me on the day she and Ty were at Zane's. We were never alone at the photoshoot and it's beyond time for me to bond with my bestie. I don't have time to give her all the details of our trip now, and we'll need a weekend together just the two of us to delve into everything that's gone down over the past several months, but for now I only need her to know the basics.

A plethora of "I'm sorry's" and "I miss you's" follow and just like that, all is right in my world again.

"After everyone leaves, can Jace and I stay to talk with you?" I stop us in the hallway before we join the others. "We're super jet-lagged, but I think it's important for the four of us to clear the air. I think the thing between our guys might be holding up LTZ stuff."

Zoey nods furiously. "Absolutely. We have to."

We hear Carter clinking a glass and we rush out to find him proposing to Lianne. Finally. Or, I should say, she finally says yes.

All of us crowd around the happy couple, except Ronni who stands to the side, furiously typing on her phone. Connor calls her name. She holds up a finger to stall him for a second, and he doesn't look thrilled.

Jace catches my eye and raises an eyebrow. I join him. "What's up with them?"

"Business," he mouths.

"On Christmas Eve?" I whisper.

We both shrug.

I lean into him, keeping my voice soft. "We're staying to have a drink with Ty and Zoey."

His brow furrows. "We've been up for nearly twenty-four hours. Can't it wait?"

"No." I see Ty watching us. "I don't think it can."

We manage to stay awake through dinner. And dessert. I almost begin to regret wanting to stay when it doesn't seem like anyone is leaving. Finally, Ronni tugs on Connor's sleeve and they make a move. Zane, Fiona, and Mia follow. Carter keeps Ty chatting until Lianne and Zoey gently guide him out the door.

Leaving just the six of us.

"Will it be weird if I nurse him?" Zoey wrinkles her nose. "Or, you guys can start and I'll come out in a bit."

I cup her shoulder. "Of course not. Please do whatever you need to do."

"I'll get Ollie." Ty raises his hand and waves before disappearing into the bedroom, returning minutes later with his tiny son. "Lena's passed out on the bed."

Jace yawns. "I'm not surprised. I haven't had jet lag in a while. It's no joke."

"Let's sit in the living room." Zoey leads the way and settles herself on the couch. Ty sits next to her, and she leans back on him as he places Oliver in her arms. Ty carefully covers them with a blanket while Zoey situates her son to feed.

They're so beautiful.

Jace and I sit opposite them. He loops his arm around my shoulder. We all sit around with goofy grins on our faces.

"I'm sorry," we all say in exact unison.

Ty strokes Zoey's hair. "No, I'm the one who's sorry. Alex, I never wanted my shit to come in between the two of you. Zoey always wanted to be there for you. If it wasn't for me and this little guy…"

"Shhh." She looks up at him. "You could never come between us, Ty. I told you that."

"Never," I echo.

Jace shifts a bit. I know this is uncomfortable for him. "I've not said this, and it's long past due. Congratulations on Oliver, my brother."

"Thanks, man." Ty smiles.

"Jace, I hope you know that I'm not mad at you for not calling me back. You were doing for Alex what I did for Ty. And if the situation were reversed, it would be the same. Alex and I are sisters. Our love for you guys just enhances the situation. We can raise our families together. Go through things together." Zoey looks over at me. "Whether we're together every single day or go months without contact, that bond is always there. It's always strong."

"I'd like to think our bond is just as strong." Ty directs the comment to Jace.

He nods. And nods. Then looks up at Ty. "I've been a bit of a dick. Obviously, we were going through a lot. When you started acting, uh..."

"Distracted? Strange? Self-involved?" Ty offers.

"Yeah, all those things." Jace chuckles. "I just couldn't fathom having to deal with more shit."

"You don't have to." Zoey tilts her head.

Ty kisses her temple. "She's right. I can deal with my own shit. I've told you many times you're off the hook, Jace. You need to take yourself off it."

I stifle a giggle. Ty's nailed it. "He likes to make sure everyone is taken care of, it's his blessing and curse."

Jace looks at me and arches an eyebrow.

"It's true," I insist.

"I'm glad you took care of Alex when she needed you." Zoey takes Oliver out from under the blanket and begins to burp him. "It gave me so much comfort knowing the two of you could rely on each other. I guess what I'm hoping is you can see Ty and I have each other's backs too. We're not going to drag you into our problems ever again."

"Okay." Jace nods.

"Okay?" Ty confirms.

"Yes. Okay." Jace stands and holds out his hand to LTZ's singer.

"So, we're gonna reconvene in the new year." Ty's question is actually a statement.

"Yeah. Alex and I have decided to bring Jen and Becca in as partners at the ranch. We finished our therapy certifications while we were in Italy, but we don't want to run that type of business on a day-to-day basis. Eventually? Sure. For now, we want Lena to grow up with her family. Which includes LTZ." Jace sits next to Ty. "You're my brother. I will always have your back, even when you annoy the fuck out of me."

"Wanna hold your godson-in-law?" Zoey holds Ollie out to Jace.

He takes the baby. "Hey, little dude. Don't you dare get any ideas about Lena. She's too old for you." He looks up at me and winks.

How amazing to be sitting here with my best friend and our husbands. It's still funny to me that this is real life for us. Married to the rock stars we worshipped from afar. With kids. Going through experiences together, both good and bad. It's incredible.

"Can I hold him?" I hold out my arms.

Jace sniffs Oliver's head and then brings him over to me. "The baby smell. It's fucking awesome."

I take my godson and look down at his sweet face. Of course, I can't help but think about the baby we lost when I hold him. It doesn't hurt, though. He's perfect. He'll be in my life forever. And, who knows? Maybe someday Jace and I will decide to adopt. Or foster. I'm not sure.

For now, we're going to focus on ourselves. And Lena. And build a life that allows us all to follow our dreams.

Because if there's one thing I've learned over the past year or so?

If you open your heart and soul?

The possibilities are limitless.

Epilogue - Four Months Later

ALEX ROLLS OVER AND stretches her arms high above her head.

A dusky-pink nipple pokes out above the sheet. Unable to resist, I lower my lips to her breast and suck. Then blow a little puff of air on it, watching it pucker even tighter. My dick is rock hard. I grind it against Alex's hip. She squirms and her eyes slowly blink awake to find me watching her.

"Mmmm." She rakes her fingers through my hair. "I love waking up like this."

I peel the duvet down to expose her other breast. Then repeat.

Alex writhes against me as I lave her tits.

One hand snakes into her panties. Slowly, I circle her clit with my index finger until she starts to get wet. Alex and I are rediscovering what pleases her because sex is not quite as it used to be. Still fucking awesome—it's us, after all—it just takes a little longer to get her going.

Sex. Side effects. Hormone balance. Diet.

We're working through all of it.

Together.

It's phenomenal.

"Are you going to fuck me?" Alex flings the linens off her body, baring herself to me. Her scar is still very red and I kiss it. Lick it. Pay special attention to the one inch raised ridge where Dr. Madison cut into her.

"You don't need to do that every time." Alex presses on my head so I'll go lower.

I look up at her as I pull her panties off. "I will kiss the scar that saved your life every fucking time."

Placing her legs over each shoulder, I bury my face in her sweet pussy. I didn't mind eating her out when she had cramps, Hell, I enjoyed it. Making Alex come would be an excellent full-time job.

It's so much better, though, when she's not hurting. When she can just lay back and enjoy what I do to her.

"Oh, gawd. Yeah," she moans when I nibble on her clit.

I insert two fingers and find her ridge. Go higher. Press. She clenches her thighs around my ears. Her stomach tenses and releases. I wiggle my tongue on her clit and swirl, pressing against her inner walls with the tips of my fingers.

"Oh. Oh. Ohhhhh." Alex arches back on her elbows and clenches hard and then floods my mouth as she comes. She doesn't scream, but her entire body shudders and writhes. I don't let up. I'm going for the multi-orgasm record. It's fitting for a day like today.

By the time she comes for the sixth time, her entire body is like jelly. Her clit is throbbing. The bed is drenched. I decide to go easy on her for the grand finale. I slip inside her and roll my hips, grind against her public bone. She bites her lip because I'm hitting her exactly in the magical spot. I take both of her hands in mine and bring them above her head, never breaking pace. "Come one more time, Poppy."

Her eyes catch mine. "You're not supposed to even be here this morning."

"What? And miss fucking my bride on our wedding day?" I swivel my hips to keep her mind on the task at hand.

She clenches her teeth and her eyes close when she gets there. Her pussy clamps around my cock so tightly I can't help but let go. I spurt inside her forever before I, too, become a satiated noodle and collapse next to her in my childhood bed.

"Your entire family heard us," Alex admonishes. "It's not like I can stop coming when you do that thing to me. How am I going to face your mom?"

I pull her against me and kiss her nose. "Worth it."

The entire clan is in town for our wedding. The band. My family. Alex's. In a few short hours, we'll get married in the grand ballroom here, in Jace's parent's house. Sure, Valentine's Day is generally a stupid holiday to get married. Then again, we're already married so when Lena picked the day, how could we say no?

"How was Ronni?" I pull on my joggers when I get out of bed.

Alex pulls the covers up to her neck. "You'd never know anything was wrong."

"Connor still won't talk about it." I grab my socks and T-shirt off the ground. "We all tried to get it out of him. Nothing."

"Will it affect anything?"

I shrug.

"Well, today's going to be epic. Did you see my dress?" She points to a garment bag hanging on the back of the door. "You might as well take a look. You've already fucked your bride."

I pretend to unzip the bag and Alex comes flying at me. "I was just kidding!" I laugh.

"This came out amazing." She traces my fresh ink, courtesy of my sister, Jordan. A Sleipnir, or eight-legged horse in Norse mythology, is thought to transport souls into the afterlife. It's fitting because the Sleipnir is most meaningful to travelers and athletes—equestrians, especially—as well as those who have lost loved ones.

My tribute to the baby we lost and to the life we've built spans shoulder blade to shoulder blade.

I spin her around and pull her hair up. Alex has a smaller Sleipnir inked at the base of her neck. "My sister doesn't win all those awards for nothing."

"Well, now I'm addicted." Alex rolls her eyes.

I open the door to leave. "I have no problem with that."

Two hours later, I stand in my black tux watching my beautiful bride descend the ballroom stairs in a white slip dress adorned with giant watercolor poppies. Her hair flows in long waves down her back. Lena, who's wearing a matching dress, holds her mother's hand as they walk toward me. My bandmates are my grooms-men. Zoey and all of our sisters are Alex's bridesmaids.

Just over a hundred of our closest friends and family attend our ceremony in my parents' opulent home.

No one knows about our secret wedding, the one Alex and I had just for ourselves in Italy. That day was just for us. To help us heal. To cement our commitment. It's a sacred day, and I'm quite sure we'll take it to the grave.

Today's wedding is for everyone whom we love. For everyone who's supported us. And it's a glorious day.

Later, after eating the feast prepared by Fiona and Ty, dancing until our feet hurt, cutting the ten-tiered cake, Alex and I are ready for our honeymoon.

What nobody knows quite yet, it's also going to be our babymoon.

Our baby is due in three days. We'll be there for the birth. Before Alex had her initial surgery, Dr. Madison extracted some viable eggs. Just as a precaution. When the unthinkable happened, it was the one hopeful thing that got us through. Gave us strength to face the tragedy. Blessedly, it didn't take long before we found the perfect surrogate.

"Are you ready?" Alex's eyes dance with excitement. "I'm so excited, I can hardly stand it."

I look at the woman for whom my love has no limits. No boundaries. No restrictions. I hold out my hand to her. "I've never been readier. Now, Poppy. Love of my life. Let's go meet our son."

***

"Did you seriously think sending me a *text* telling me you'd give me a *divorce* was gonna fly with me? God, you LTZ guys and your stupid goddamn notes." ...Connor & Ronni's Encore is next up in Fearless Encore.

For all things Kaylene, sign up for my mailing list.

Behind the Scenes

Limitless Encore Edition

Holy moly!

This was quite a journey. Alex and Jace are such a special couple, and they were very closed lipped about their story. I had to prod and cajole it out of them.

After all they're private people, right?

I'll let you in on a little secret. I always knew I would be writing these Encore books, and in my mind Jace and Alex's story was in the can. I knew EXACTLY what they were going to face and how they'd meet the challenge.

Then I started to write.

And no. The story I had planned for them just wasn't theirs to tell.

If you've been following Less Than Zero (and if this is your first book, here's a little inside info), you'll know that Alex is the character inspired by my very best friend in the world. She and I have been friends since I was three and she was four. Not just friends, though. Best friends. In every single sense of the word.

Sisters.

That's not to say we haven't had time apart where we don't talk every day because let's face it—life happens! We lost touch for a bit in college. When we reconnected, then we saw each other all the time. From watching bands during the 90's in the Seattle music scene, to getting into a lot of mischief, to ghosting David Copperfield (yes, there's a story there), our adventures have known no bounds. We've been through romances, marriages, divorce and everything in between. There's no one on this planet who knows me more than she does.

I must mention, Cavalia is our very, favorite show in the entire world. We always attend together. We always sit in the front row. We cry like babies because it is the most beautiful thing in the world. I hope that they tour again. I know that COVID shut them down for a while, but I'll be there in the front row again the minute they do.

So, this is not just a story about Jace and Alex. It's also a story about BFFs and how friendships can ebb and flow and remain solid even in the face of adversity and tragedy. How your BFF, and the solid feeling that he or she is ALWAYS there for you is and can be one of your great relationships.

Hopefully this was conveyed with the respect and love it deserves, because aside from my husband, my bestie truly has my heart and soul.

Now let's get to the love story—

As I mentioned in ENDLESS Encore, my plan to delve deeper into these couples is super fulfilling to me. I hope you're enjoying the follow-up love stories of our favorite LTZ couples as much as I love writing them.

One of my favorite things about Alex and Jace is their dynamic. What started out as a schoolgirl crush on a hunky older rockstar drummer has turned into a love so solid, true and deep that it is, truly, limitless.

If only Alex can open her heart to Jace. If only she can learn to let go of her fears. If only she can learn how to be vulnerable and let him take care of her. Show her he'll be there for her no matter what.

Then she has no choice.

As with ENDLESS ENCORE, I wanted to share more about Jace and Alex's background story to give you more depth to who they are and how they've come to this point. Some of my closest friends have had horrific health issues, and it takes such a toll on a couple and their families. For someone as active and healthy as Alex?

Devastating.

So – before I go, I must give a special shout out to one of my closest friends in the world, Julia. She is probably the smartest person I know (she's both an OBGYN and a Lawyer!). Her help in going through all of Alex's health issues was imperative – I had to get it right. Every time I'd run into a "snag," I'd text her and she'd answer me right away. When I delve into a topic that is so important and so sensitive, meticulous research is very important. Not just for you as a reader, but for me and the integrity of the story I want to tell you. Anyway, Julia is a badass, and I appreciate her soooo much.

I hope you enjoyed Alex and Jace's story. Got a little more insight into the rest of the gang. Another perspective. And, beyond all else, an epic love story with a hopeful HEA. A story of how love knows no limits.

Two more ENCORES to go, and then I have a couple of new series in the works that will spin off from our Less Than Zero world...

Thank you for reading,

Love,

Acknowledgments

This book was an absolute labor of love, and I couldn't have done it without the help and support of the following awesome rock stars:

Cover Designer/Graphic Designer/Finder of Hotties: Regina Wamba

Editor: Grace Bradley

Formatting: Willow Yanarella

PR: Dani Sanchez, Wildfire Marketing

Agent: Stephanie Phillips, SBR Media

Website Maven: Sherri Kiarsis, Ruby Moon Designs

My Right Hand: Willow Yanarella

Model(s): Garret McCall (@mrmcmodel) and Carson Hunstad (@carsonhunstad)

My VIPs/Alpha and Beta Readers - Anna, Beth, Kris, Sheila and Willow

OMG! To the ARC readers, bloggers, bookstagrammers & my Street Team – I can't do this without you.

Thank you thank you thank you for helping spread the word—I'm overwhelmed by your love, support, kindness, etc. Thank you for making my dream come true!

Dax and Violet Morgan appear courtesy of the phenomenal Lauren Rowe. She's an amazing writer and one of my great inspirations.

Dedication

This is dedicated to all of my friends who have suffered health issues and infertility. It takes strength and resilience to navigate, and I'm in awe of you. You know who you are.

About the Author

KAYLENE WINTER IS AN best-selling author of steamy, contemporary romance.

Each character-driven novel is filled with snappy dialogue, pop-culture references and enough steam to make you fan yourself. Kaylene weaves authenticity, emotion and angst into a turbulent rollercoaster ride of love, passion and soul-searing romance always ending with a delicious HEA.

Kaylene lives in Seattle with her amazing Irish husband and her Pomsky, Phalen. She loves creating art of all kinds.

Other Titles